Other Books by the Author

THE VOICE THAT SPEAKETH CLEAR $3.50

HISTORY OF the teaching of the classics at the University of Pittsburgh.

TROY AND HER LEGEND *(illustrated)* $3.50

FRESH INTERPRETATION of the legend of Troy as it has been retold through the ages in literature, painting, ceramics, tapestry, sculpture, gems, coins, and opera.

LEGEND BUILDERS OF THE WEST
(illustrated) $4.00

BEFORE THERE WERE written records to preserve the significance of the human scene, it was recognized in mythology, and men ever since have striven to extract and mold this record of human experience into the patterns of their own times. The constantly growing fund of experience drawn from mythology and contributed to it by artistically and spiritually resourceful men has made it a medium to reveal with increasing clarity the spectrum of life's varied significance.

Dr. Young, author of *Troy and Her Legend* and *The Voice That Speaketh Clear,* here concerns himself with the transmission of classical mythology through the arts of the West. The nine legends he discusses have found receptive climates and varied interpretations through many forms of communication.

ECHOES OF TWO CULTURES

The publisher acknowledges with gratitude the gift of the Robert S. Marshall Memorial Fund for Classics

Story of Lucretia. Translation of Valerius Maximus by Simon de Hesdin and Nicolle de Gonesse (1469). Bibliothèque Nationale *fr.* 284, folio 176

Echoes of
Two Cultures

Arthur M. Young

UNIVERSITY OF PITTSBURGH PRESS

A token of my warm esteem for
Dean Stanton C. Crawford

τῶν τότε ἀρίστου
καὶ φρονιμωτάτου
καὶ δικαιοτάτου

Contents

LIST OF ILLUSTRATIONS

PROLOGUE

The theme of this book is the transmission of two cultures through legends. The process of transmission is not the handing of a corpse from one age to another, but the dynamic relay of an echo through the canyons and recesses of Western annals. For airwaves of culture die only in a sterile setting. Alive, they pick up their own sounds in the social cultures they strike, and reverberate on and on.

> Forward steps in art . . . are the result of the
> imitation of and admiration for beloved predecessors.
>
> Pasternak, *Doctor Zhivago*

The carriers in the ancient legends selected as illustrations of the theme are two semi-historical personages: Cyrus the Great from the early Greek world, and Lucretia from the early Roman world. Both stories introduce from their respective societies the theme of transgression of rights: in one against a people, and in the other against an individual. In both, a woman's courage and determination bring an offender to his rightful doom. In the process of retribution, however, though both were innocent, Tomyris, Queen of the Massagetae, was crushed by the loss of her son, and Lucretia, wife of Collatinus of Latium, herself chose not to survive the loss of her honor.

The Greek champions of freedom in the fifth century B.C. saw an inexorable and divinely ordained law of ethics, imposed upon the overweening transgressor, as an object lesson in the philosophy of history. The Roman champions of freedom were motivated by a solemn respect for the sanctity of their homes and their women. The stories of Cyrus and Lucretia, both, came from great-souled social contexts where high dignity lifted history into tragic drama, and brought both under the jurisdiction of ethics.

The political and personal ethics in the two stories, born of stern resolve, were not lost in the West, nor were the memories of the two women who held the transgressors accountable under their high sense of propriety. As long as men fall into covetousness and lust, the import of the two stories is clear in its reminder of the need for discipline and of the dire effects of lack of discipline. The story of Cyrus, in various versions now partly lost, was transmitted through the Greek tradition to the Latin, and as the Mediterranean basin was assimilated by Roman culture it was expressed in the two languages. The sources in which the story of Lucretia was transmitted to Livy from the third and second centuries are all lost. But her story too became bilingual. With Greek and Latin as carriers the two stories became a part of the total Greco-Roman cultural experience, which was transmitted to the Latin-Christian tradition of the early Church and the Middle Ages. The complexity of the late Middle Ages gradually evolved into the Renaissance, with a broader pattern of living and a rebirth of old skills. Through the long twilight, the darkness and the dawning, both stories retained a usefulness amid the changing culture of the West, and artists kept the stories alive in succeeding generations. In spite of the broken fabric in the tradition of the stories certain story tellers carried it even when it lost its historical individuality. Some of these story tellers were Valerius Maximus, the Christian Fathers, Orosius, Jordanes, Dante, Petrarch, Boccaccio, the *Gesta Romanorum*, Christine de Pisan, Machiavelli, and Bandello. In England, Lydgate, Pettie, and Shakespeare retold both stories.

The ancient body of experience was often, in the long history of European culture, a superior body of experience. Its didactic value was never lost. The broad expression of

Renaissance and post-Renaissance culture in their various arts drew generously from the ancient experience. History, drama, and social values were all superbly combined in the stories of Cyrus and Lucretia. As woman assumed the complimentary mantle of romance, there were elements in both stories which responded to the new concept of her. Her sterling qualities of mind and soul, and even her body as the bearer of those qualities, called forth new expression in the arts. The two stories grew in the creative imaginations of those who sought expression through them, and they found their fulfillment in the fulfillment of the societies which nurtured them.

It is the purpose of this book to piece together the record from the broken fabric of the ages, as its dismembered parts, lodged in museums, libraries, memories, and skills of the present, can be remade and envisioned from this distant point of historical perspective. The classical impulse was central and continuous. Through the ages it was confirmed, supplemented, and modified by the dominant spirit of other times. Though new expressions of it came with new historical impulses and new instruments and skills, the ever-changing and growing culture of the West stayed long in the orbit of the classical impulse and was guided by its magnetism.

The Story of Cyrus the Great

HERODOTUS

Cyrus the Great (*ca.* 598–528 B.C.), king of Persia, magnetizes the first book of Herodotus' *History* into unity. The rise and fall of Cyrus is the large epic theme of the book, validating in part the adjective *Homerikotatos* (most Homeric), applied to him by the literary critic Longinus (13.3). Herodotus inquired into the cause of the struggle between Greeks and "barbarians," (*i.e.*, non-Greeks). The Persian chroniclers laid it to the Phoenician abduction of Io from Argos. Similar reprisals followed on both sides in this perennial outdoor game of men. Herodotus pronounces those who engage in it as being either scoundrels or fools (1.4). Taking his tongue from his cheek he singles out the man who first inflicted injustice on the Greeks—Croesus, king of the Lydian Empire. With epic deliberateness Herodotus reviews the successive kings of Lydia, closing his account with the fall of Sardis in 546 B.C. and the capture of Croesus by Cyrus the Great. Condemned to be burned alive on a funeral pyre, Croesus was miraculously saved by a change of heart by Cyrus and by a cloudburst sent from Apollo, upon whom Croesus had called for deliverance. Herodotus then reviews the rise and fall of the Median Empire down to king Astyages, from whose daughter was born its doom—Cyrus of Persia. Herodotus' account of Persia coincides with Cyrus' rise and fall, and brings him within a page of the end of the first book.

Herodotus (*ca.* 484–425 B.C.), called the father of history by Cicero (*Laws* 1.1.5), has immortalized Cyrus the Great in the consciousness of the West with his memorable accounts of the birth and death of the founder of the Persian Empire.

Astyages, king of the Medes, had a dream about his daughter Mandane which disturbed both him and his wise men. For the dream seemed to portend the doom of the Median Empire. The king accordingly married his daughter not to a Mede, but to an unaspiring Persian, Cambyses. Within the year Astyages dreamed of a vine growing from the womb of his daughter and overshadowing all of Asia. Since Mandane was close to the time of birth of her first child, Astyages kept her in confinement, and when the child was born he ordered Harpagus, a trusted courtier, to slay it. Harpagus, finding himself in a position of mortal danger if he either slew or failed to slay the little boy, decided to let someone else do it. He therefore summoned Mitradates, a herdsman of Astyages, and ordered him to expose the boy in the mountainous pastures infested with wild beasts. The herdsman's wife was named Spaco, which in Greek, comments Herodotus, would be "Cyno," connoting a dog. Mitradates went home with the child and a heavy heart. During his absence his wife had been delivered of a still-born child. He told her of the tension in the home of Harpagus, of the baby dressed in golden raiment, and of his discovery that it was the royal child. His wife begged her husband to substitute her child for the abandoned one, thereby giving her own a royal burial and the royal child a chance to live. The suggestion seemed good, and was carried out. After seeing a corpse of a child, Harpagus' agents were satisfied that the master's order had been carried out. As a result of these circumstances the prince was raised in humble estate.

The identity of the prince was uncovered ten years later. The herdsman's adopted son had been elected king by some boys at play, and proceeded to assume that role in earnest. A son of a nobleman, for refusing to carry out his assigned task, was whipped by the boy-king. The irate father protested at the court, and at the hearing which was arranged the boy-king startled the real one by defending his action. Astyages was quick to surmise that this might be his grandson, and the threat of torture brought the truth from Mitradates. Harpagus, when confronted with the newly-discovered set of facts, related truthfully to the king what he had done, and why. The king appeared pleased because his grandson had been spared, and he asked Harpagus and his only real son to join him in a thank-offering for the occasion. At the banquet Harpagus was served the cooked and dismembered body of his own son, and later was shown the hands, feet, and head. He was allowed to carry the remnants home, presumably for burial.

When Astyages consulted the wise men for further advice, all agreed with him that in all likelihood the dream regarding his grandson had now been innocently fulfilled; so Astyages permitted the boy to return to his real parents, Mandane and Cambyses. On his way home the boy learned of his true parentage. Whenever he spoke of Cyno, his foster-mother, as he often did, Mandane and Cambyses, in order to associate the boy with divine providence, spread the rumor abroad among the Persians that the boy had been saved from death by a nurturing dog.

Meanwhile, Harpagus craved revenge, and regarded Cyrus as the avenger. When he believed that he had prepared the Median nobles for revolt, Harpagus sent to Cyrus a message sewn in the belly of a hare. With a clever ruse of pointing out to them the difference between hard toil and feasting Cyrus persuaded the Persians to revolt, and Harpagus successfully arranged to have the Medes defect to the cause of Cyrus. Astyages had the wise men impaled for their advice to him and in battle was defeated. And so, after his reign of thirty-five years the kingdom fell into the hands of Cyrus. Harpagus had a chance to gloat over the fallen Astyages, but Cyrus permitted his grandfather to live out his days (Her. 1.107-130).

Within less than a century after his death Cyrus had already gathered around himself a mantle of legend. The Greek sources upon which we must rely for our knowledge of him come from a myth-making age, with the capacity to create and the will to believe within a great framework of experience. The peculiar contribution of genius in the context of these given facts is not to record them, but to illuminate them with perceptions, convictions, values, and tangible creations which not only bear the impulse of a given age, but also reveal a sense of common humanity and progress.

Herodotus, aware of four versions of Cyrus' career (1.95), chose the one which in his judgment rejected exaggeration and arrived at the truth. According to Tertullian (*On the Soul* 46), Charon of Lampsacus, author of a *Persian History*, and regarded by Tertullian to have been a predecessor of Herodotus (*Herodoto prior*), anticipated Herodotus in his report regarding the dream of Astyages concerning his daughter. Tertullian had read Herodotus' account of both dreams. Herodotus was aware of a report that a miraculous incident had saved the life of Cyrus at the time of his exposure, but he preferred a rational accounting for the incident. But if the life of the royal child was as charmed as the story has it in his miraculous escape from death and the early recognition of his identity through the emergence of inborn qualities from outwardly humble circumstances, then, indeed, it is time for the logographer and the annalist to give way to men of faith, imagination, and romance. The similarity between the events purportedly attending the births of Cyrus and of Perseus, the traditional progenitor of the Persians, has been pointed out.[1]

In the visitation of *ate* (calamity) upon *hybris* (arrogance), in the retribution which caught up with Astyages for his ruthless condemnation of a grandson and his sadistic punishment of one who prevented it—all working through the victims of this *hybris*—, oriental history provided Greek thought and Greek artistic expression of the early fifth century with a profound case study of God's interest in humility and due propriety. The outcome of events suggests that the divine plan was more interested in the Greek virtue of *sophrosyne* (propriety in behavior) than in the revelation of itself through dreams as a substitute. Those who preferred divination to ethics were not thereby exempt from ethics. Man's effort to foresee the plan of destiny through the interpretation of dreams often, ironically enough, actually hastens the plan because of his unsuspecting reliance on a misinterpretation. In his *Eumenides* (534) Aeschylus pronounced *hybris* the child of irreverence. Euripides after Herodotus' time permits Hecuba to state that Zeus, advancing over a long and silent path, leads mortal affairs in accordance with justice (*Trojan Women* 887f.).

Cyrus' magnanimity in sparing Astyages (Her. 1.130)—and later Croesus—marks him as a forerunner of a constantly refreshed Hellenic awareness of the need for compassion in the changing affairs of men. But Croesus, who was brought down from his pinnacle of wealth and power by Cyrus, and then magnanimously spared by Cyrus and a miraculous rainstorm, with the best of intent toward Cyrus and, therefore, with fateful irony, gave advice to Cyrus which led to his downfall. Herodotus saw the hygienic social value of the birth and early life of Cyrus as he reported them. He must be admired for his desire to search—the basic meaning of the Greek word *historia* —into both the facts of history and their larger meaning.

Herodotus found most plausible the version of the death of Cyrus the Great which was by tradition inflicted on him by Tomyris, queen of the savage Massagetae. In the darkest of times, subsequently, in the West, this queen was remembered when even Herodotus was forgotten. The Massagetae were an uncivilized people living east of the Caspian Sea and northeast of the Persian realm. Cyrus, intoxicated by victories and under illusions of greater-than-human destiny, coveted the realms of the Massagetae. When his ruse of a specious offer of marriage with the widowed queen failed to obtain his end, Cyrus made preparations to force a crossing of what Herodotus calls the river Araxes. Tomyris advised him to abandon his designs on unoffending neighbors, but assured that he would not do so, she offered Cyrus his choice of battlefield, on either his or her side of the river. Cyrus' Persian counsellors advised him to choose a site in his own territory, but his captive counsellor Croesus, once the proud lord of the Lydian Empire, as though he were a chorus in a Greek tragedy, first warned him that the affairs of mortal men are subject to the vicissitudes of a fickle wheel of fortune, and then outlined to him strategic reasons for preferring a battlefield on the enemy's territory. He suggested the stratagem of leaving in camp the worst troops and a sumptuous repast of food and drink as an easy means of overpowering the foe. Cyrus, accepting the advice of Croesus, made the necessary arrangements with Tomyris, the enemy's queen. Her son, Spargapises, led a detachment of one-third of the army against the Persians. He had no trouble in overpowering those whom Cyrus had left behind. But sleep followed the repast of the enemy, and the returning Persians slaughtered some and captured others. Among the captives was Spargapises. Tomyris reproached Cyrus for his dishonorable deed. She gave him a fair chance to restore her son and leave her land, unharmed. Otherwise, she swore by the Sun, the god of her people, that she would give this bloodthirsty man his fill of blood.

Cyrus ignored her words. Spargapises upon awakening was filled with shame. When Cyrus acceded to his request to remove his shackles, the boy committed suicide.

The ensuing battle is reported by Herodotus to have been the fiercest the "barbarians" ever fought among themselves. The Massagetae finally prevailed. The greater part of the Persian army was destroyed, including Cyrus himself, after a reign of 29 years. His body was brought to the queen. She decapitated him and dipped his head in a bucket of human blood, to fulfill her warning. Yet she realized the tragic irony of her situation, that the death of her son turned her moment of revenge into ruin (Her. 1.205-214).

This story of Herodotus also well represents his interests. He was impressed by the heroic, epic, and chivalrous woman. The fierce vindictiveness of the Oriental ruler in matters pertaining to human life he often notes. But above all both Herodotus and the age in which he lived believed in a momentous guidance of its affairs by supernatural forces whose ultimately beneficent intent was to humble the proud and ambitious. In this story those whose heads are lifted too high are brought low, and they share in the disaster which they inflicted upon others.

God in his jealousy, Herodotus states in another context, smites the arrogant transgressor (7.10e). Isaiah, long before Herodotus, and Horace, long after him, made solemn pronouncements on the subject. Croesus had learned of plans bigger than his own in the misery of his own experience (*pathemata . . . mathemata gegone*, Her. 1.207). The chorus of the *Agamemnon* of Aeschylus in the previous generation had uttered the same dire message: *pathei mathos* (177). In this story, therefore, history is the record of a divine plan at work to achieve among men humility through humiliation. Even the instrument of the plan's accomplishment, Tomyris, was crushed by the loss of her son—himself an innocent, though foolish, victim caught in the toils of retribution.

TOMB OF CYRUS

Two centuries after the death of Cyrus, Alexander the Great, standing at the violated tomb of Cyrus, read the inscription thereon:

O man, whoever you are and from wherever you come, . . .
I am Cyrus, founder of the Persian Empire. Begrudge me
not, therefore, this little earth which covers my body.

In his biography of Alexander (69), Plutarch observes that Alexander was deeply moved *(empathe)* by this inscription with its reminder of the uncertainty and precariousness of human affairs. In recent years the word "empathy" has had a considerable vogue to indicate sensitivity in projecting one's self into the situation of another. A century before Plutarch's time the Greek geographer Strabo (15.3.7) mentions a visit of Alexander to the tomb of Cyrus at Pasargadae, where also his palace was, and confirms at least the substance of what

Plutarch later wrote about the epitaph and the tomb. As Orosius observes, with a kind of *basso profondo* reminiscent of Byron, in his brief sketch of Sardanapallus, king of Assyria:

> In qua brevitate pensandum est: quantae ruinae cladesque gentium fuere, quanta bella fluxerunt ubi totiens tot et talia regna mutata sunt (1.19.3).

> Amid this fleeting scene one is compelled to reflect on the number of failures and disasters among nations there have been; how many wars have come in steady stream wherein so often so many and such kingdoms have gone their way.

After these 2,500 years it should be of interest at this point to visit the tomb of Cyrus with one who has recently been afoot in that part of the world. Mr. Byron found it "a sarcophagus of white marble on a high, stepped plinth, standing by itself among the ploughed fields. It looks its age: every stone has been separately kissed, and every joint stroked hollow, as though by the action of the sea. No ornament or cry for notice disturbs its lonely serenity. Enough that Alexander was its first tourist. There used to be a temple round it. One can still see how this stood from the bases of the columns. Since then, it has become the Tomb of the Mother of Solomon. In deference to this transformation, a miniature mihrab and an Arabic inscription have been carved on one of the inside walls."[2]

MEMORIAL VERSES

From antiquity there survive a number of memorial verses, either questionable in origin or spurious, regarding famous people. Among them are quatrains concerning both Cyrus and Tomyris. The one memorializing Cyrus runs as follows:

> Quantum fata valent atque inmutabilis ordo
> astrorum docui Cyrus, quem nulla domare
> vis potuit, non Astyages Babylonve superba,
> Massagetis tandem me fata dedere tremendis.[3]

The power of Fate and of the unchangeable order of
the stars I, Cyrus, have made manifest, whom no force
could overcome, neither Astyages nor proud Babylon.
But at length Fate surrendered me to the dread
Massagetae.

RELIEFS AT BISITUN

A series of gigantic reliefs cut into the side of a mountain at
Bisitun in Iran in the third year of Darius' reign, 518 B.C.,
recounted the achievements not only of Darius, but also of his
predecessors, Cyrus and Cambyses. Beneath and around the
reliefs was inscribed their story in old-Persian cuneiform char-
acters. The reliefs, 60 feet long, and the inscriptions, were first
closely inspected by Rawlinson in 1837. In order to study the
magnificent historical record he hung precariously supported
by ropes 300 feet above the floor of the valley. Above him
rose the 2,000-foot cliff facing an old caravan route through
Persia.[4] Here, high above the heads of men, was a magnificent
record of the rulers of the Iranians, who came into Persia
about 1100 B.C.

CTESIAS

Ctesias was physician at the royal court of Persia for a few
years at the end of the fifth century B.C. As an historian he was
in a favored position because he knew the Persian language,
lived at court, and had access to the royal archives. His two
accounts of Persia and of India—the former a history of the
Orient in 23 books, beginning with the foundation of the
Assyrian Empire—are known to us mainly because of a lengthy
résumé of their contents made by the Byzantine scholar
Photius in the ninth century, and still extant.

Ctesias is in sharp disagreement with Herodotus with
regard to Cyrus. He, who may himself be in a bad position to
throw stones, accuses Herodotus of mendacity and of telling
tall tales *(logopoion)*. Aristotle (*Generation of Animals* 756b)
also categorized Herodotus as a spinner of yarns *(mythologos)*.

On the other hand, Aulus Gellius (*Attic Nights* 9.4.3) lists Ctesias himself among Greek writers of strange yarns and fantastic, incredible stories. Lucian, master of tongue-in-cheek satire and parody, accuses Ctesias of "talking through his hat" on matters pertaining to India, which he had never seen or heard of reliably.[5] Lucian's *True History* (2.31) includes a visit to an island of brimstone, sulphur, and dire punishment, the worst of which went to such fabricators of lies as Ctesias and Herodotus. And in Lucian's essay on *How to Write History* (39) Ctesias is accused of allowing himself to be a mercenary tool of the Persian emperor, in contrast with true historians such as Thucydides and Xenophon.

Ctesias maintained that Cyrus had no family relationship with Astyages. According to him, when Astyages fled before the attack of Cyrus, a follower of Cyrus by the name of Oebaras subjected to torture the daughter of Astyages and her husband to find out where Astyages was. Thereupon Astyages, to spare them such pain, surrendered to Cyrus; but he, nevertheless, held Astyages in high honor and married his daughter, thus becoming his son-in-law rather than being his grandson.[6] Later, however, (whether with the approval of Cyrus or not is not recorded) Oebaras is reported to have prompted a eunuch close to Cyrus to abandon Astyages in the desert, where he died and was buried.[7] The Greek orator Isocrates (*Evagoras* 38), a contemporary of Ctesias, is our sole authority for the statement that Cyrus assassinated his maternal grandfather. During a campaign against the Derbikes, reports Ctesias, Cyrus suffered a wound and died.[8] Prior to the battle of Thermopylae, Artabanus is reported by Herodotus (7.18) to have reminded Xerxes of the fateful expedition of Cyrus against the Massagetae. On the other hand, the Greek chronicler Diodorus, who in the mid-first century B.C. had access to important historical documents no longer available to us, states that the queen of the Scythians took Cyrus prisoner and crucified him (2.44.2). Ctesias,[9] and Dinon in his *Persian History*,[10] as well as Justin centuries

later, estimated the reign of Cyrus at 30 years, one year more
than the calculation of Herodotus. St. Jerome in his commentary on Eusebius' *Chronicle* (book 2) estimates a reign
of 30 years;[11] and Jordanes, of 32 years.[12] The Oebaras mentioned by Ctesias appears in the text of Justin as Sybares.

DINON

The *Persian History* of Dinon, who may be placed around
the middle of the fourth century B.C., also attributed low
birth to Cyrus. Astyages' uneasiness about this underling in
his palace was aroused when Cyrus made a journey back
to Persia. The ominous prediction of an impending menace
made by a bard confirmed Astyages' misgivings about Cyrus.[13]

XENOPHON

Cicero (*Brutus* 112, 281, 282) commends Xenophon's
Education of Cyrus (*Cyropaedia*, about 361 B.C.) as a fine
work still read in his day. The impetuousness, however, of
the historical Cyrus and his tragic end Cicero thought to be
a poor substitute for the qualities of dignity, humility, indus-
triousness, and modesty. Had the young Crassus, he continues, not forsaken those qualities to emulate Cyrus and
Alexander, he might have avoided the doom which befell
both him and his father (at Carrhae in 53 B.C.). In his eulogy
of Cyrus, Xenophon pays little attention to historical records,
more of which were available to him than now to us. In world
literature the *Education of Cyrus* is part of the literature of the
ideal prince. Xenophon's work is a romance woven around an
historical figure. According to Xenophon, Cyrus died as
serenely as he lived, with noble words of counsel on his lips.
The political philosophy which Xenophon endorses and the
social *mores* which he attributes to the Persian ruler reveal
in the early fourth century a general disillusionment regarding the "democracy" of Athens, and an attachment to the
discipline of the few and the philanthropy of one. Both
Xenophon and Plato saw in the wise and humane ruler—but

each on his own specifications—a better solution for the
common people than they could provide for themselves.
Xenophon's thinking on the subject, based undoubtedly on
his experience in, and admiration for, Persia and Sparta, the
younger Cyrus and Agesilaus, then rose above history into
the ideal and the romantic. The aspirations of great art often
carry it beyond the bounds of literal historical veracity: Tasso
and Gibbon follow their own separate objectives in treating
the first Crusade. The *Education of Cyrus* is an extravagant
tribute to a life the nobility of which has left many echoes
in both Xenophon's time and subsequent eras.

STRABO

Strabo was a much-travelled geographer and historian contemporary with Augustus. He was born in and of the Hellen-
ized East, then a part of the Roman world. He brought history
into the realm of books, libraries, personal observation, travel,
curiosity, and common sense. Though he shared some of these
traits with Herodotus and professed to surpass him in them,
yet he lacked the great soul and the excitement of the momentous found in Herodotus, who also came from Asia
Minor. Strabo complains of the unguarded credulousness of
his predecessors in matters pertaining to the Caspian area,
and of their love of tales *(philomythian)*. He professes to
place more reliance on Hesiod, Homer, and the tragic poets
than on Ctesias, Herodotus, Hellanicus, and others (11.6.
2-3); and yet he himself was poorly informed about the
geography of the very area concerning which he attributed
looseness to his predecessors. For whereas Strabo and others
before him thought that the Caspian Sea was connected with
the northern sea (2.5.14), Herodotus states correctly (1.202-
203) that the Caspian Sea was an independent body of water.
The Laurentian Library in Florence has a Latin translation
of Strabo's Greek manuscript made by Guarino Veronese and
Giorgio Tifernate, dedicated to Paul II, and printed in Rome,
in 1469 by Sweynheym and Pannartz.

NICOLAUS OF DAMASCUS

A lost element in the transmission of the period covered by Herodotus' first book was the *Universal History* of Nicolaus of Damascus, a philosopher-historian and friend of Augustus, written in Greek. His long historical treatise survives only in fragments. With the same deliberateness as Herodotus he proceeded from the Assyrians and Medes in his first and second books, to the Lydians in the fourth and sixth, and to the Medes and Persians in the seventh. For the history of the Medes he followed Ctesias.

Nicolaus reported that Cyrus was of very humble birth, the son of Atradates. Through fine, inborn qualities, however, he rose to the position of wine-bearer of Astyages. His mother, a shepherdess, related to him a dream which she had while still pregnant, that a stream from her would flood all of Asia. According to both Ctesias[14] and Nicolaus the daughter of Astyages was married first to a Spitames, and only later to Cyrus. Having met Oebares under a good omen, Cyrus took him as a companion. In the war which developed between Cyrus and Astyages the Persians withdrew without victory to join their wives on a mountain peak at Pasargadae. When reproached by their wives, who taunted their men and exposed themselves, they returned to battle and killed 60,000 of the foe. Cyrus thereupon ascended the throne of Astyages, now a captive.[15] Also, a fragment of Nicolaus' work survives in which Croesus fell into the hands of Cyrus.

VALERIUS MAXIMUS

As the Roman government lost control of the Mediterranean basin in the early Christian centuries, both Greece and the Greek language slowly faded from the consciousness of the West. The oblivion of Greece, once the curtain was drawn, was almost total and lasted for a millennium. Herodotus was carried into the Middle Ages in the West through a Latin tradition, often with no association with his name and no reflection of his superb narrative power. Historical writing in either the western or eastern Mediterranean ceased to be an independent sphere of activity in its own right, but its record, when available, remained useful to lexicographers, grammarians, epitomists, theologians, rhetoricians, and moralists. Herodotus served the classical commentators and the Latin Middle Ages as a parson. Often only his frock was available, and it needed little recutting to befit its new environment and morality. One of Herodotus' best stories is this about Cyrus, but unfortunately, it was not to be available for a long time in the West in its own right.

One of the many documents which was destined to keep alive the *History* of Herodotus during the Middle Ages is the anthology of historical anecdotes compiled for use in rhetorical training and as moral *exempla* by Valerius Maximus, of the time of the Roman emperor Tiberius. Valerius cites Tomyris as an example of revenge (9.10. *ext.*1). The name of Tomyris will survive in various spellings, but it will be easily recognizable. Valerius Maximus needs only a scant four lines to reduce the story to its essentials: the horrible deed of Tomyris, Cyrus' insatiable thirst for blood, and his share in causing the death of her son. The story is disengaged from its broader context of divine involvement in the affairs of men. Few ages have felt this as profoundly as that of Herodotus or Aeschylus. The source of Valerius Maximus for this story was probably Pompeius Trogus. This collection of anecdotes was very popular during the Middle Ages as a source of instruction in both school and sermon. Valerius' place in the didactic tradition of Roman heroes is recognized.[16] Two even shorter versions of the manuscript were made by later writers. With the invention of printing, the manuscript was published by 1471, and many editions made it available throughout most of Europe before the end of the century.

SENECA

The Roman philosopher Seneca in the first Christian century commented providentially (*On Anger*, 3.15.1) on the
sadistic act of Astyages, who served at table the bodies of
Harpagus' sons to the father, then inquired of the father how
he liked the dish, and when he saw the father's mouth full,
bade the heads of the sons to be brought. The pathetic father,
in a state of stunned paralysis, helplessly replied, "At the
board of a king any meal is pleasant." Pending the condemnation and punishment justly due, commented Seneca,
anger, words, and grief must be checked. Such is conviviality
and converse in the presence of kings. Amid one's own
destruction one is compelled to laugh. (Funeribus suis ad-
ridendum est.) The classic expression of the situation of
hiding one's doom in laughter is the tragic Pagliaccio (Canio)
in Leoncavallo's opera, who with heart crushed by the awareness of his wife's infidelity forces himself to go on stage and
act the clown whose role he plays, and to hide in laughter the
sighs and tears of his deepest emotions.

In words which take on charged meaning in the light of
Seneca's tragic end in the last fitful years of Nero's reign
Seneca finds no justification of continuing to live a life of
servitude in a context of a concentration camp *(ergastulum)*.
With a Lucretian scorn he asks why fools moan over their lot
when there are many avenues of escape into freedom (of
death) through the precipice, the sea, the river, the well, the
tree, the throat, heart, and vein. Nero allowed Seneca to
choose the form of his death. For those who wish to share
his last hours Tacitus (*Annals*, 15.61-64) tells the story. The
philosopher regarded suicide as his privilege, and, under
certain specific conditions, as preferable to life. The Christian
fathers, if at times inclined to accept Seneca as one of their
own, would in this point disown him.

Aeneas Silvius Piccolomini (Pius II) wrote a long epistle entitled *On the Miseries of Courtiers (De Curialium Miseriis)*, the source of three of our earliest English eclogues of Alexander Barclay. Aeneas Silvius seems to have followed Seneca in attributing sons, instead of a son, to Harpagus, whom he mistakenly called, as in one manuscript of the text of Seneca and in the text of Orosius, "Harpalus." Aeneas Silvius also attributed this fiendish act to Cyrus, king of the Persians, instead of to Astyages (chap. 32). In this mistake he may have been trapped by a vague relative pronoun and unexpressed subject in Seneca. In this connection Seneca, Justin, and Orosius use the gerundive of the verb *epulare*, the only variation being in the number of the form.

FRONTINUS

In his *Stratagems* Frontinus refers to the fortunes of Cyrus. In this Latin work of the period of Domitian the distinguished general and statesman, best known for his careful superintendence of, and report on, the water supply of Rome, gathered examples of military strategy from the records of history. He relates, as do also Herodotus, Justin (1.6.4-6), and Polyaenus (7.6.7), the method by which Cyrus induced the Persians to throw off the Median yoke. For after a day of cutting timber and a day of feasting the Persians were quick to prefer the latter to the former. Cyrus reminded them that the first day symbolized the conquest of the Medes, and the second day freedom and happiness, and that the second goal could be reached only through the first (1.11.19).

Frontinus also relates briefly the strategy of Tomyris in overcoming Cyrus' army, despite her lack of superiority in forces. Pretending fear she lured him into a defile known to her army, and defeated him by exploiting the advantage of her natural position (2.5.5). A comparison of the text of Frontinus in these two passages with that of Justin reveals nothing of significance. Printed texts of this work of Frontinus became available around the middle of the sixteenth century.

Clemency of Cyrus. Miniature by Jehan Foucquet. Translation of Josephus' *Jewish Antiquities.* Bibliothèque Nationale *fr. 247*

Tomyris and Decapitation of Cyrus. Christine de Pisan, *Epistle of Othea to Hector.* Bibliothèque Royale de Belgique, *ms.* 9392, folio 6ov.

AULUS GELLIUS

Aulus Gellius, a Roman author of the Antonine period of the Empire who lived in Athens on different occasions, was familiar with the text of Herodotus, and attempted to assign an exact date to his birth (*Attic Nights* 15.23). He calls Herodotus *homo fabulator,* "a spinner of yarns" (3.10.11).

JOSEPHUS

Flavius Josephus, a participant and historian of Jewish affairs, who wrote in Greek in the late first century of the Christian era, states in his *Jewish Antiquities (De Antiquitatibus Iudaeorum* 11.1) that Cyrus in the first year of his reign, recognizing his heaven-sent destiny as told in the Hebrew prophets, proposed to restore the Jews to their homeland and to rebuild their temple. To that end he directed that funds be contributed.[17] St. Jerome in his commentary on *Isaiah* (12.44)[18] refers to the honor in which Cyrus was held by the Jews, as one chosen by God to do His will. He adds an historical note that the foundations of the temple were laid in the reign of Cyrus and that the temple itself was begun by his successor Darius. He cites the eleventh book of Josephus' *Jewish Antiquities* for the reverence felt for Cyrus by the Jews, and refers his readers to the *Education of Cyrus* by Xenophon.[19] Jordanes in the sixth century knew of the good services of Cyrus in repatriating a large number of enslaved Jews in their homeland and in planning a new temple for them.[20] And in the eleventh century the monk Hervaeus Burgidolensis called Cyrus a "shepherd of God" *(pastor Dei)* and an agent of divine will, for releasing the people of Israel from captivity.[21] Such information could have reached the Latin Middle Ages from Josephus, for Latin translations of his writings after the sixth century were widely diffused in the Middle Ages—a mark of his popularity. The earliest surviving Greek manuscript of Josephus is much later than the Latin.

The continued popularity of Josephus in the Renaissance is exemplified by a magnificent manuscript of his *Jewish Antiquities* of the early sixteenth century in the Bibliothèque Nationale in Paris (*fr.* 247). The manuscript is adorned with miniatures and illuminations of great beauty which are now associated in part with Jehan Foucquet, a now highly regarded painter and miniaturist of the fifteenth century. One of the masterpieces of volume 1 is the frontispiece to part 11 illustrating the clemency of Cyrus. The Persian king is crowned and enthroned. A marble portico supported by Corinthian columns opens into a paved court adorned with a Roman triumphal arch bearing sculptured reliefs, and with a Corinthian column supporting a warrior. Beyond the wall is a landscape containing a gabled house and a castle, both reminiscent of Foucquet's native environment, the valley of the Loire River. Around Cyrus stand his courtiers. A group of Jews kneel before him. Out of his clemency he will permit them to return to their country and to rebuild their temple at Jerusalem. Foucquet spent a considerable time in Rome, and so brought back to the France of his time the excitement of the flowering Italian Renaissance.[22]

Josephus also reported the tradition that Cyrus died in his war against the Massagetae (11.2.20).

POLYAENUS

Polyaenus was a Macedonian rhetorician of the second century after Christ. His orientation was, of course, Roman. He compiled from many sources both known and lost today, and often uncritically, a collection of stratagems and examples of wisdom, bravery, and cunning. It is a lifeless work, and did not deserve, and since written in Greek was not able, to exercise any great influence on later times in the West. His brief section on Tomyris (*Strategemata* 8.28), an example of cunning in women, reverses the story as reported by Herodotus. For according to Polyaenus, Tomyris, fleeing in simulated fear with her troops, left behind a camp well-stocked with wine, food, and victims for sacrifice. The Persian force exercised the historic right of the victor to make unstinting use of what it found, in a night of revel. While the Persians lay in drunken slumber, Tomyris had no trouble in destroying them.

LUCIAN

The brilliant Greek satirist Lucian makes a passing reference to Cyrus' shocking fate. Mocking mythology Lucian asserts that Hermes learned of the impending decapitation and blood-bath of Cyrus from a revelation by Clotho, the spinning Fate (*Charon* 13).[23]

AELIAN

Aelian was a Roman rhetorician of Italian stock who lived in the third century of the Christian era and wrote in Greek. His *Medley of History (Varia Historia)* is a compilation of anecdotes and excerpts culled during his wide reading of Greek literature. He mentions Herodotus (2.41). His allusion to the suckling of Cyrus by a dog (12.42) gives him an opportunity to list other children of legend who were suckled by animals. The myth-making age of Greece has found in Aelian its literate undertaker.

POMPEIUS TROGUS, JUSTIN

Another of the carriers of history during the long eclipse of Greek in the West was the *History* of Pompeius Trogus, now known through an anthology made by Justin. Pompeius Trogus lived in the time of Augustus, and Justin a century or more later. Important Greek texts, now mostly lost, such as those of Theopompus, Timaeus, Clitarchus, Polybius, and Posidonius, lay behind the work of Trogus, and he brought to history respectable qualities of mind and a lively style. The first writer to mention Justin was St. Jerome. Justin is generally not neglected in the medieval literary lists of England. During the Middle Ages, Pompeius Trogus was known almost exclusively through Justin, and an abridgement of Justin's work was also widely read. Boston of Bury in the English Middle Ages mentions Pompeius Trogus and his pupil *(discipulus suus)*. He took an entry from Vincent of Beauvais, but misunderstanding Vincent he put Trogus in the time of Ninus. Justin's work is not mentioned by Boston, but Boston again erroneously calls Justin Martyr (a different Justin) "Trogi Pompeii abbreviator."[24] Since the original Latin document of Pompeius Trogus was an extensive treatment of the area controlled by Alexander the Great, and began with Ninus, founder of Nineveh, Cyrus and Tomyris found their rightful place in the document.

Justin's account (1.4.1-1.7.1) of the early days of Cyrus' life begins with Astyages' dream of a vine which grew from the womb of the only daughter of Astyages, and which was to darken all of Asia. Because of the ominous interpretation put on the dream by the interpreters *(arioli)* Astyages gave his daughter in marriage to Cambyses, a Persian of humble station *(mediocri viro)*. The task of slaying the child born to her was assigned to Harpagus, characterized as a privy-counsellor of the king *(regis . . . arcanorum participi* and later *ministro)*. The logic of the situation prompted Harpagus not to slay the child personally, but to entrust the exposing of it to a herdsman of the king. By chance a son had been born to the herdsman's wife at that very time. She successfully importuned her husband to let her see the royal child. When the herdsman returned to the forest to get the child, he found it being suckled and protected from beasts and birds by a dog. Justin's text is as follows:

> Eius igitur uxor, audita regii infantis expositione, summis precibus rogat sibi perferri ostendique puerum. Cuius precibus fatigatus pastor reversus in silvam invenit iuxta infantem canem feminam parvulo ubera praebentem et a feris alitibusque defendentem (1.4.9-10).

His wife, therefore, hearing of the exposure of the royal child, made the warmest entreaties that the boy be brought and shown to her. Wearied by her entreaties, the herdsman, returning to the forest, found a dog beside the child offering its udders to the little fellow and protecting him from beasts and birds.

The herdsman was moved by the same pity which moved the dog, and when he brought the child home, the dog also solicitously followed! The mother held the boy in her arms, and was rewarded with such a coaxing smile, to say nothing of her joy in the child's robust appearance, that she begged her husband to substitute her own child for the royal baby. He complied. The child's new mother and nurse *(nutrici)* was hereafter named *Spargos* from the Persian word for dog. The spelling of the word varies among the manuscripts.

In his new humble environment the child was called Cyrus. Later, when chosen by lot as king by his playmates, Cyrus imposed a flogging on the rebellious *(contumaces)*. The irate parents complained to the king. An interrogation of the boy led to surmises, and the confession of the herdsman established the identity of the boy. The wrath of Astyages was vented not on the herdsman or on the child, but on Harpagus, in a way familiar to all who know the story.

But biding his time and driven on by revenge and sorrow *(dolore orbitatis admonitus)* Harpagus told his tragic tale to Cyrus in a letter urging Cyrus to attack the Median Empire. The letter was sewn into a hare, and reached Cyrus through a trusted messenger posing as a hunter. Cyrus was also encouraged by a dream to attack, but at the same time was forewarned to enlist as an ally the first man he met on the morrow, who turned out to be one Sybares, a Persian enslaved by a Mede. Cyrus revealed to his people the choice of destiny that lay in their hands by giving them a day of toil as lumberjacks and a day of feasting. Preferring the feasting to the toil they gladly followed him on the road to freedom from Median rule. Harpagus, entrusted with the command of the Median army, immediately surrendered to Cyrus. Astyages made a last effort with the forces which remained to him. To the men in his front ranks he gave the choice of either breaking the line of the enemy before them or of being cut down by the army behind them. The front lines, of necessity, fought for survival. While the Persian line was gradually breaking, the mothers and wives confronted their men, begging them to return to battle. As the men wavered, the women lifted their garments and exposed themselves, asking whether the men wished to return to the wombs of their mothers or of their wives. Thus reproached the men returned to battle and routed their opponents. Astyages was captured, but Cyrus, acting as grandson rather than as victor, merely deposed him, and placed him in charge of the Hyrcanians, since Astyages did not want to return to the Medes. The Hyrcanians later fought under Xerxes at Thermopylae. Justin estimated the duration of the Median Empire at 350 years; Herodotus, by a different calculation, at 128 years. Sybares, who shared Cyrus' adventures as a result of the latter's dream, Cyrus placed over the Persians, and married him to his own sister.

The differences between the two versions of the story as recorded by Herodotus and Justin are many. In terms of length Justin reduced the story to one-third of the version of Herodotus. Justin, like Pompeius Trogus before him, dispensed with quoted dialogues. Pompeius Trogus had criticised Livy and Sallust for this practice of embellishing historical records (Justin 38.3.11). Apparently he would not have appreciated Byron's tribute to Livy's "pictured page" (*Childe Harold's Pilgrimage* 4.82). There is less concern in Justin about dreams and their validity. Whereas Herodotus is specific in assigning names, Justin is not. Strange proper names are difficult to preserve in a text, and they cease to be important. In Herodotus' account Mandane was married to Cambyses because of Astyages' dream of a stream of water flooding the whole of Asia; it was the second dream, of the vine darkening Asia, that led to Astyages' decision to slay the child. In Justin's account there is only one dream, that of the vine, which led to the marriage of the daughter to Cambyses. Herodotus' version is more humane in having the child of Mitradates and Spaco born dead. Whereas Justin relates that the herdsman found a dog suckling the young Cyrus in the woods, Herodotus, though he knew of a story that the infant Cyrus had been suckled by a dog in the mountains, adopted this as a rational explanation for the legend about the boy. In Herodotus' version the shepherd learned the identity of the child on the way from the palace and brought him directly to his home. The two versions differ regarding the time of naming Cyrus. In Herodotus' story the boy presumably received the name Cyrus after he was returned to his real parents; but in Justin's account the child received the name while with his foster-parents. Strabo (15.3.6) states that Cyrus, whose name had been Agradatus, took the name Cyrus from a river. Justin makes no reference to the hands, feet, and head of Harpagus' son, which in Herodotus' version were brought to the father after he had eaten his child. And in Herodotus' version Cyrus asked the Persians to report to him with their falchions, that they might clear a field; but in Justin's version the Persians were asked to come with their axes to clear a forest around a road. The incident of the women exposing themselves as a means of persuading their men to resume battle against the Medes is not found in Herodotus' story. On the other hand, the interview between the avenged Harpagus and the fallen Astyages is not found in Justin's story.

The account of Justin (1.8) concerning the struggle between Cyrus and Tomyris differs in certain details from that told by Herodotus. The queen's decision regarding the battlefield was based not so much on generous chivalry and total confidence in her invincibility as on calculated military strategy. The retreat of Cyrus, reported to be frightened, the banquet, and the wine are still in the story. The queen sent her young son, who is not named, with one-third (as in Herodotus) of her troops to pursue the foe. The son is characterized as being ignorant of military strategy, because he turned into a banquet what was to have been a battle. Cyrus returned during the night and killed all of the Scyths, including the queen's son. In Herodotus' account the son was merely captured by Cyrus, and took his own life from shame when released from chains. Now motivated solely by a desire for revenge, Tomyris proved herself superior to her foe in trickery. For, feigning a loss of nerve (*diffidentia*) because of a wound, she executed a planned retreat which lured the over-confident Cyrus into a defile, the tactical advantage of which she had already explored. Two hundred thousand Persians were slain with their king. Not even a messenger survived the disaster. The comfort of revenge followed as the queen uttered the insulting taunt, "Sate yourself with the blood for which you ever thirsted insatiably." The element of epic magnanimity and chivalry found in Herodotus' account is here missing, as also any supernatural involvement. Justin's account allows people of power to live and die within a formula defined by themselves, sometimes reaping the whirlwind in consequence of sowing the seed. The military catastrophe reported by Justin would have served well the more reflective people who clothed Cyrus in the garb of early fifth-century Greek ethics.

AMMIANUS MARCELLINUS

Ammianus Marcellinus was a fourth-century man of affairs, traveler, historian, and satirist. Though a Syrian Greek, he wrote in Latin a history of the Roman Empire from the end of the first century to his own time—an enlightening document for students of antiquity. He points out the weakness to which Cyrus' arrogance and ambition reduced the Persian Empire, and records the annihilation of Cyrus' army by Tomyris, queen of the Scythians (23.6.7). The original "son" of Tomyris for whom the queen sought revenge has become

"sons." The story is here in the hands of an otherwise preoc-
cupied soldier, and has lost its artistic form and its significance
as part of a divinely ordered universe.

ST. AUGUSTINE

A French translation and commentary of St. Augustine's
City of God, about the year 1478, by Raoul de Praelles has
an illuminated miniature on folio 187 under chapter 7 of book
4. The miniature portraying the story of Astyages, Mandane,
and Cyrus is based on the commentary; the text at this point
consists only of an historical reference to Cyrus.[25]

Another translation and commentary of the same work by
the same translator, of the year 1480, contains two miniatures
on this story: In one Astyages in full regalia, even to the
crown on his head, dreams of a vine emanating from his
daughter and covering all of Asia; and in the other the infant
Cyrus is carried off to the woods for exposure. An inscription
in letters of gold has recorded the traditional name of "Spaco"
as "Spartacus!" The manuscript is now in the Bibliothèque
Municipale of Mâcon, France, and is a derivative of the same
manuscript in Paris (Gaucourt) to which the Hague-Nantes
St. Augustine was indebted.[26]

ST. AMBROSE

The catastrophe that goes with high position gave an ur-
gency to a knowledge of history among the Christian fathers.
The transition from Herodotus to them was easy, for the catastrophe pointed to the need for humility in both. The subject led St. Ambrose (*ca.* 340–397) to Cyrus in one of his
letters.[27]

For all his high position Cyrus became a subject of mockery
before the power of a woman. Ambrose was very familiar with
the violence of Cyrus' death and the contempt with which he
was treated. Pompey and Hamilcar also confirmed for Ambrose the historical pattern of the fruits of pride.

OROSIUS

The Spanish Christian chronicler Orosius wrote nothing regarding the birth and childhood of Cyrus. In two short sentences Cyrus had already proclaimed war on his grandfather Astyages. The revolting act of Astyages in serving to Harpagus at dinner the body of Harpagus' only son is noted without any motivation being attributed to Astyages, but as motivation for the defection of Harpagus to Cyrus. The remoteness of this material to the Middle Ages is apparent in the manuscript reading of "Harpalus"—quite another historical figure—for "Harpagus." Orosius includes the incident found in Herodotus regarding the basket, whereby Astyages assures himself that Harpagus is fully aware of the horror of his plight upon seeing the head and hands of his son. Orosius' account includes, as does that of Justin, the threat of Astyages to cut down from behind any of his front ranks who yield from fear. The word *necessitas* (compulsion) is common to both accounts. A comparison of the texts of Orosius (1.19.9-10) and of Justin (1.6.13-17) will reveal the method of composition of the former writer. Both authors at these points in their narratives state that the mothers and wives of the Persian army exposed themselves physically before their men in order to shame their men into battle, and they tell how Cyrus treated Astyages after conquering his army. Aside from the omission of what probably was one line in the text of Justin (*nepotemque . . . egit*, 1.6.16) Orosius has lifted the whole passage almost verbatim from Justin.

Orosius too closely followed the story of Tomyris as found in the text of Justin. He gives two reasons for Tomyris' decision to allow Cyrus to cross the Araxes: one of them implied in the text of Herodotus, namely, her self-confidence, and the other found in the text of Justin, namely, the tactical advantage of getting a river behind her foe. Simulated fright on the part of Cyrus in retreating from the battlefield is mentioned by both Justin and Orosius, but no motive for the retreat is assigned by Herodotus. Justin writes that Cyrus returned by

night; Orosius merely writes "later" *(mox)*. Both authors agree
that Tomyris resolved to assuage her grief with blood, not
tears; that she feigned a loss of nerve *(diffidentia),* because,
writes Justin, of a wound, and Orosius, of dejection over her
losses. The word *insidiae* is used in both texts to denote the
trap set for Cyrus. The word *angustias* (narrows) adds a further detail in Justin's account, and *montes* in Orosius'. The
failure of even a messenger to survive is noted by both authors,
and they also observe through their phrase *non muliebriter*
the absence of feminine weakness in Tomyris. Her imprecation over her fallen foe, as other details, is almost identical in
both authors, as follows:

> Satia te, inquit, sanguine, quem sitisti, cuiusque
> in satiabilis semper fuisti. Justin

> Satia te, inquit, sanguine quem sitisti, cuius per
> annos triginta insatiabilas perseverasti. (Orosius
> 2,7.6)

The sibilation alone expresses her contempt. As late as 1788
Lemprière's widely read *Classical Dictionary,* in its account
of Cyrus, used the first part of this imprecation of Tomyris in
its Latin form. The Laurentian Library in Florence has a
parchment manuscript in uncial letters of the sixth century of
the first six books of Orosius' *History.* The manuscript is the
earliest extant text of Orosius, and was the earliest manuscript
in the personal library of the Medici *(plut.* 65.1). The text of
Orosius became known in England through the translation
by King Alfred.

SIDONIUS APOLLINARIS

Sidonius Apollonaris of Lyons, a fine example of Christian
humanism in the fifth century, knew of Cyrus' miraculous
escape from death thanks to the nurturing of a dog, and of his
insatiable greed and cruelty. This slayer of 200,000 men was
finally brought to bay in the confines of a Scythian valley. A

bereaved queen introduced him to a blood-filled skin (*Carmen* 9.30-37).

BOETHIUS

Gibbon (*Decline and Fall,* chap. 39) called Boethius "the last of the Romans whom Cato or Tully could have acknowledged for their countryman." He was executed in the early sixth century by Theodoric. His *Consolation of Philosophy,* a medley of prose and verse, is one of the world's best pieces of prison literature, and the last flowering of pagan literature. In the second book of the *Consolation of Philosophy* Boethius recalls his reading of Herodotus, without mentioning him, or feeling he had to mention him. The goddess of Fortune, who visited him in prison, reminded him of the wheel on which human affairs turn, and of the reversal which brought Croesus from the pinnacle of good fortune to the brink of death at the hands of Cyrus (2.2).

JORDANES

Jordanes wrote his *Gothic History* around the middle of the sixth century.[28] The shadows have by now, indeed, fallen over the record of the past. And Cyrus' downfall has ceased to bear an artistically conceived and divinely directed tragic message. Jordanes mentions Pompeius Trogus, but does not follow his (and Justin's) account of the queen's victory over Cyrus. His source may be regarded as Cassiodorus' lost history of the Goths, which Jordanes abridged in this work. Tomyris was the queen of the Getae, a people whom Cyrus hoped to conquer. She permitted Cyrus to cross the Araxes, and preferred to overcome him in battle rather than to take advantage of a strategic position. Jordanes reports two battles: one in which the Parthians destroyed most of the army led by the queen's son, including the son, and the other in which the queen in turn overwhelmed the Parthians and took much loot. The queen then founded on the shore of the Black Sea the town of Tomi, naming it after herself. It was at Tomi near the sea that the Roman poet Ovid spent his last sad years in exile.

The self-confidence of Tomyris, as implied by Herodotus, is stated by Orosius and Jordanes. Tomyris' desire for strategic position, however, is rejected by Jordanes as her reason for allowing Cyrus to cross the Araxes.[29]

ISIDORE OF SEVILLE

Isidore of Seville, an outstanding antiquarian, encyclopaedist, and churchman of the early seventh century, wrote the *Origines*. Benighted as this work may be in many respects, yet it is one of the important instruments of transmission for classical culture from its fountains in the ancient world to its recovery in the Renaissance. Isidore acknowledges Moses as the first non-pagan writer to record history from the early beginnings. Among the pagans he recognizes first the Phrygian Dares' account of the Trojan war. The document which is now extant under the name of Dares, *History of the Fall of Troy (De Excidio Troiae Historia)*, may actually be a work of the sixth century after Christ. Among the Greek writers considered to follow Dares, Herodotus is recognized as the first (1.42.2). It is an oasis to find his name recorded. The name "Massagetae" Isidore derives from the people called "Getae," who are *fortes, i.e., graves, i.e., massa* (9.2.63)!

HUGO OF FOLIETO

A rarity, indeed, in this period is the mention of Herodotus by name. Hugo of Folieto of the early twelfth century, in his work *On Marriage* (*De Nuptiis*, 1205B), mentions Herodotus, apparently in connection with the story of Candaules and Gyges.[30]

PETRUS COMESTOR

Peter the Voracious (Petrus Comestor or Manducator), a much-used and much-praised French scholar of the late twelfth century, received his sobriquet from the multitude of books he devoured. His associates urged him to write a lengthy book to which they might go in the interest of ascertaining the truth of history *(pro veritate historiae consequenda)*.[31] His masterpiece was the *Historia Scholastica,* an exegetic and historical commentary for the Scriptures. In writing his commentary he made use of certain pagan writers and of Josephus, whose works in Greek still survive and were available in Latin translation during the Middle Ages. Such authors as Origen, St. Jerome, St. Augustine, Hesychius, and especially Isidore of Seville were among his sources. Petrus may have had a slight knowledge of Greek. His horizon included both Greek and Roman antiquity and the Persian Empire.

The circumstances attending the birth and childhood of Cyrus are reported at some length in the *History* of Petrus.[32] The Herodotean account is seen dimly through the mist of the intervening centuries. In Petrus' version Astyages married his daughter to a common soldier *(militi plebeio).* The roles of Harpagus and of the herdsman Mitradates are, in substance, still in the medieval version. Neither of the two men, however, is named. Harpagus started out in the text of Justin with his name spelled correctly. The manuscripts of Orosius call him "Harpalus." Now he is reduced to anonymity. In the text of Justin, Harpagus is called *regis arcanorum participi* (privy counsellor of the king, 1.4.6), and *ministro* (aide, 1.4.7). Petrus calls Harpagus *cuidam participi arcanorum.* It is clear that Petrus has been using Justin. Petrus also calls Harpagus the king's *secretarius,* a medieval word defined as *consiliarius* (counsellor) by a scholiast. Mitradates is not named by either Justin or Orosius. In Justin's text he is called *pastori regii pecoris* (shepherd of the royal flock, 1.4.7), and in Petrus' text *uni de pastoribus regis* (one of the king's shepherds).

Petrus now follows the text of Justin. The shepherd exposed the child as he had been ordered to do, and then came home to his wife and newly-born baby. The wife persuaded him then to make the substitution of babies. Neither Petrus nor Justin states that the shepherd's child had died, a Herodotean detail. When the shepherd returned to the forest to get the royal child, he found that a dog was nursing it and protecting it from the beasts and birds. They therefore named the child "Sparticus" (puppy), for the Persians call a dog "spartos." For purposes of comparison the texts of Petrus and Justin are supplied, as follows:

> Invenit Canem[33] praebentem ei ubera, et a feris et avibus defendentem. Cumque tulisset eum ad uxorem, allusit ei tamquam diu notae, vocavitque puerum "Sparticum," id est "catulum." "Spartos" enim Persica "canem" sonat. (Petrus)

> The herdsman found a dog offering its udders to the child, and protecting it from wild beasts and birds. When he had brought the child to his wife, it played with her as though she had been known for a long time, and she called the boy "Sparticus," (puppy). For "spartos" is the Persian name for "dog."

> Invenit iuxta infantem canem feminam parvulo ubera praebentem et a feris alitibusque defendentem. (Justin, 1.4.10)

> [The herdsman] found near the child a dog offering its udders to the little boy and protecting it from wild beasts and fowl.

Later Justin writes *veluti ad notam* adlusit (1.4.12).

> [The child] played as though with one who was known.

Thus an association with a dog enters the story in all accounts: in the versions of Herodotus and Justin through the name of the foster-mother, and in the version of Petrus through the name of the child and the incident of its having been suckled by a dog. According to Petrus, Cyrus acquired the name "Cyrus" when the Persians acclaimed him their king, for, he says, the word means "heir" *(haeres)*.[34]

There are other similarities in the texts of Petrus and Justin. Petrus states that Cyrus, acting as boy-king, punished the rebellious and disobedient *(contumaces et inobedientes)*. Justin (1.5.2) also uses the word *contumaces,* whereas in Herodotus Cyrus had asserted his authority over the son of Artembares, a Mede of distinction. The reply of the boy-king in defending his action before Astyages is expressed through the same phrase by both Petrus and Justin, as follows:

> Ille intrepidus se ut regem fecisse respondit. Petrus

> Ille ..., cum nihil mutato vultu fecisse se ut regem respondisset... (Justin 1.5.3).

In Petrus' account Astyages turned his newly discovered grandson over to Harpagus, who was told by the grandfather only that the child was the son of a shepherd. In Justin's account no position was taken on the matter, but presumably from the context the child was returned to his parents, as Herodotus explicitly stated.

One curious incident in the version of Petrus is found in Justin (1.6.13-15) and followed verbatim by Orosius. When the revolting Persians fled under the attack of Astyages, the wives and mothers of the Persians appeared on the scene, exposed themselves before their husbands and sons, and asked the men whether they wished to return to the wombs of their mothers and be reborn. In shame the Persians returned to the battle and were victorious. But though Petrus and Justin have reported the same incident, yet Petrus has largely restated it in his own words.

Petrus very briefly summarizes the horrible death of Cyrus (col. 1474, chap. 19). If he allowed himself to deploy as a narrator of the period of Cyrus' childhood, he becomes merely an annalist in reporting his death. But he knew that Cyrus was defeated in battle by Tomyris, and that he was beheaded and subjected to the blood for which he had long thirsted. The sibilation of her insulting remarks expresses her final contempt:

> Satiare sanguine quem sitisti.

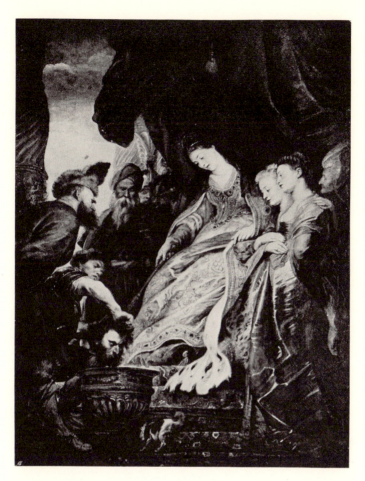

Tomyris and Cyrus. Rubens. Louvre, Paris

Childhood of Cyrus. Tapestry by Jacobo van der Goten. Santa Bárbara, Madrid

The incident of the queen's son is not included. Petrus reckoned the reign of Cyrus at 30 years. Here, then, in the historically-oriented interpretation of the Scriptures by a medieval Christian we have a clear indication of the process by which an ancient Greek experience was transmitted from Greek to Roman antiquity and into the Middle Ages.

DANTE

In *Purgatory,* Vergil and Dante saw the souls of those who were atoning for their pride under a burden of heavy stones. The two poets were soon confronted with the soul of Provenzano Salvani, the ambitious master of Siena and an example of the emptiness of worldly name (*Purg.,* end of canto 11). Just as Vergil and Dante had seen engraved on the white marble of a mountain's face many stories of humility (canto 10), so now Vergil asked Dante to behold on the ground wonderfully sculptured examples of fallen pride upon which those who dwell in Purgatory must gaze as they move along. Anyone who visits the old churches of Italy today will relive the experience of walking over the buried past, and Dante himself suggests the analogy. Those beneath their eyes are a neatly arranged integration of biblical and classical lore: Satan, Briareus, Thymbraeus, Pallas, Mars, Nimrod, Niobe, Saul, Arachne, Rehoboam, Eriphyle, Sennacherib, Cyrus (and Tamiri), Holofernes, and falling Troy. The allusion to Cyrus is brief, but includes space for Tomyris' contemptuous remark to the head of Cyrus:

> Sangue sitisti, ed io di sangue t'empio (canto 12.57).
>
> Blood thou did'st thirst for; take thy fill of blood.

The original story of Herodotus fits nicely into one of the central convictions of medieval Christian morality: that pride goeth before the fall. Provenzano Salvani faced a Florentine army on the field of battle in 1269. Having been defeated, he was decapitated. His head was carried high, just as the

Devil had cryptically revealed to him, but in the camp on a lance.

In his Latin treatise *On Monarchy* (2.9) Dante advanced the thesis that the Roman people established their supremacy over the world through the will of God. Many others had failed to achieve this supremacy because of their lack of divine support. In citing historical examples Dante draws, as he indicates, on Orosius, and he quotes Ovid. His third example is Cyrus, king of the Persians, upon whom Tomyris, queen of the Scythians, inflicted at the same time death and a termination of his ambition. For Dante history was a record of the working of God's will.

PETRARCH

For Petrarch (1304-1374), too, the experience of the past energized the present. For him, the first modern man, modernity carried no implication of a severance of roots. In his *Triumph of Chastity* (104-105), written in Italian, Petrarch recalls the great and memorable revenge (*la gran vendetta e memorabil*) which the widow inflicted on Cyrus in Scythia. In his *Triumph of Fame* (2.94-99) he refers again to the revenge of Tomyris on Cyrus. In an earlier version of his *Triumph of Fame* (1.148-150) Petrarch associated the greed of Cyrus for blood with that of Crassus for gold, observing that in the end both had their fill of such greed. In a rousing letter in Latin verse to Aeneas of Siena, Petrarch intimates that the Italian race in the richness of ancestral precedents (*exemplis dives avorum, Epistole Metriche* 1.3.141) may find the power and determination for a new destiny. Did not Tomyris, undaunted by the death of her son or by the tradition of her sex, carry out with the resolution of a man the heinous decapitation of her Persian foe (1.3.143-145)?

BOCCACCIO

In the last years of his life Boccaccio (1313-1375) wrote his moralizing historical work *On the Vicissitudes of Famous*

*Men and Women (De Casibus Virorum et Feminarum Illus-
trium).* Concerning the value of historical studies he wrote:

> Unde non possunt non censeri prudentissime dixisse
> qui parentem virtutis et vitae magistram historiam
> adpellavere.

> Whence they cannot fail to be thought to have
> spoken most wisely who have called history the
> parent of virtue and the teacher of life.

He mentions the power of God, who is Fortune, the frailty of
human life, and the fickleness of Fortune. The content of the
first book of Herodotus is known to Boccaccio, through Justin.
The task of exposing the infant Cyrus was assigned by Harpagus to a shepherd, who put the wailing child on an island
to be devoured by beasts. When he returned at the request
of his wife to recover the child, he found it being suckled by
a dog whose bites and barks protected the child from wild
birds. When the shepherd's wife took the child in her arms,
it smiled as if it recognized her. Thereupon she decided to
adopt the boy, later called Cyrus, and to expose her own
child. Harpagus was later punished by Astyages for his care-
lessness, for he unknowingly ate his own son's flesh, served
to him by Astyages.

A dream helped Cyrus get the help of a slave Sybaris in
his attack on Astyages, nor was the aid of Harpagus wanting.
In his hour of victory over Astyages Cyrus showed his humaneness by sparing his grandfather and giving him the pre-
fecture of Hyrcania.

Boccaccio records the trap which Tomyris successfully
set for Cyrus' army, the annihilation of the army, and the
revenge exacted of Cyrus by the queen. The royal body was
abandoned unburied to the birds and beasts.

The moralizing historian finds it difficult to believe that
divine will was not present in the fall of Cyrus *(quasi divino
nutu).* The judgment of God *(Dei iudicium)* was visited upon
Cyrus. Boccaccio was moved by his story to exclaim:

O inexcogitata mortalibus fortunae mobilitas!

O fickleness of fortune unforseen by men!

O eximium cupiditatibus nostris atque superbiis, si patiamur, exemplum, si fragilitatem nostram et Dei potentiam velimus agnoscere!

O splendid example, if we permit, for our greed and pride were we willing to recognize our frailty and the power of God!

Boccaccio also pays tribute to Tomyris in his work *On Illustrious Women,* in which over a hundred ladies receive recognition for their loyalty to human ideals and their usefulness in implementing the divine plan. Lucretia and Tomyris there stand side by side in his examples.

GESTA ROMANORUM

The *Gesta Romanorum* is an anonymous collection of moralized stories of various origins, compiled in its Latin version perhaps in the fifteenth century, and soon translated in various forms into English and the vernacular languages of Europe. Dozens, even hundreds, of manuscripts and, later, of printed editions of those stories pervaded Europe, providing for pleasure and instruction a supplement to already existing repositories of experience. It is interesting to observe that in this collection there are echoes, however faint, of the father of history. This great literary raconteur has now become a parson. One of the last dying embers of Cyrus' stratagem against Tomyris provides the dim light in which may be seen the shadow of the devil and of the sin of conviviality when fortified with intoxicating beverage. The story[35] is concerned with a stratagem of the devil in leading many to ruin: A prince who was unable to overcome his foe devised the stratagem of abandoning camp—food and all—to the enemy by feigning retreat. Amidst the repast left for a voracious enemy was a plentiful supply of drugged wine. On his return the prince killed all of the sleeping foe. Similarly, to clinch the story's intent, the devil in apparent flight ensnares those who seek conviviality in taverns. Through intoxication he leads at will into the paths of homicide and wanton living. The way to eternal life lies elsewhere. The original story as narrated by Herodotus sustained a morality within which man could well confine himself, if anyone else and eventually he too is to prosper. The adaptation of the story in the *Gesta* hardly justifies the morality parasitically attached to it.

ART OF DYING

Another popular document of the late Middle Ages was the *Art of Dying (Ars Moriendi),* a theological "Emily Post" in its area of experience. Caxton translated the manuscript from French, and printed it about 1490. Over 300 manuscripts in Latin and the vernacular languages were available, and before 1500 a hundred editions, some in woodblock, were made. Perhaps from the frequent ravages of plagues, or from the greater capacity for, and intoxication of, new areas of thought in the growing Renaissance, thoughts of dying became an obsession in the fifteenth century. A complement to the new humanism, which sought out the good life, was the interest in propriety in dying. Illustrations in Caxton's edition of the document depict decapitation as one of the grim closing chapters in the lives of the sinful. The streets of Italian cities contemporary with the document confirmed its veracity.

CHRISTINE DE PISAN

Christine de Pisan was a prominent figure in the intellectual life of early fifteenth-century France, and an exponent and example of the enlightened Christian woman and of chivalry. Her *Cyte of Ladyes,* as an early English translation has it, is a city of God for ladies provided under the auspices of Dame Reason. The author narrates the circumstances under which the city and its cloisters and walls were built, and by which "noble ladyes were ordeyned to dwell in the hyghe palayces and hyghe dongeons." Ladies of several cultures were selected for this hall of fame. The author's knowledge of Boccaccio helped her, as well as others, to select them.[36] Among those honored were Sappho, Cenobia, Penthesilea, Semiramis, the Erythraean Sibyl, Juno, Elizabeth, Thisbe, Medea, Dido, Penelope, Ruth, Rebecca, Sara, Clotilda, Judith, Paulina, Agrippina, Cassandra, and Mary Magdalene. The queen of the Amazons of Scythia, Tomyris, was a sage "by whos wytte cautele and strengthe, Cyrus the stronge and myghty kynge of Perse was overcome and taken."[37] She learned that Cyrus would attack her as part of his general plan to conquer the world. Realizing the impossibility of defeating him by force of arms she resorted to strategy. Having armed her ladies and disposed them effectively in the woods and mountains on his line of march, she allowed him to enter her territory. When he was trapped in an ambuscade, she had the trumpet sounded. The ruse was completely successful. By command of the queen, Cyrus and his barons were taken alive and brought to her pavilion. She was especially angry because he had slain one of her maidens. The barons were decapitated to provide a blood-bath for Cyrus' head. At the same time the queen brought down on Cyrus an imprecation for his insatiable cruelty. An illuminated Flemish manuscript of the year 1475, in the British Museum, contains a Dutch translation of this work of Christine. Folio 45v. portrays Tomyris as the Amazon queen with lance and hat.[38]

Christine's work entitled, in its translation into early English, *The Epistle of Othea to Hector* is a collection of a hundred stories: each containing a text in rhyme, a prose version pointing to a pertinent chivalric virtue with documentation from philosophy, and a moral application supported by quotations from the Church fathers and the Scriptures.

Story #57 in this document is concerned with Tomyris and Cyrus. Tomyris was queen of the Amazons, an undaunted warrioress and wise ruler. Cyrus mounted an invasion of her territory. After having permitted Cyrus to enter her realm, she ambushed his army in a defile and annihilated it, and him with it. She then ordered his body to be decapitated and his head cast into a barrel of the blood of his lords. Blaspheming him for being blood-thirsty, she bade him drink his fill. The author then remarks that one should not disparage the weak, for they may possess great wisdom and alertness. Plato is then used for support of this thesis. In commendation of Tomyris, whom good knights should emulate, her humility and meekness are mentioned, and St. John Cassian is used to recommend humility as the foundation of the noble work of perfection and charity. Solomon is then quoted in Latin as testimony of the value of humility before God. Tomyris has here become a champion and example of the Christian faith. One of the principal sources of Christine, especially for this story, was an early universal history of the ancient world in French, which had been in circulation since the thirteenth century.[39] Only a part of the entire story of Tomyris has found its way into Christine's text. But it was enough to sustain the morale of an age of militant Christian chivalry in France.

Manuscript #9392 of the Bibliothèque Royale de Belgique contains one miniature to illustrate each of the hundred stories in this work of Christine de Pisan. The miniature for story #57 depicts Tomyris ordering Cyrus to be decapitated. As the kneeling monarch lifts his hands for mercy, the executioner's sword is about to fall on him. Nearby is a cask of blood already containing one head.[40]

Christine's *Lavision* is a prose work in which she expresses her encyclopaedic scholarship through allegory. She sees Cyrus as a contemporary of the Greek philosophers Anaximander and Anaximenes, and of Tarquin the Proud in the Roman world. For Cyrus' conquest of Babylon she cites her sources: Orosius and St. Augustine. The hostility of Cyrus and Astyages is also mentioned in her work in verse, *The Fickleness of Fortune (La mutacion de fortune).*

TRANSMITTING DOCUMENTS
OF EARLY RENAISSANCE

The Middle Ages bequeathed to the Renaissance not only distant echoes through derived documents of a personality once vividly recorded in the pages of ancient historical documents, but also manuscripts of those documents, and scholarly tools through which the manuscripts might be used. The gradual rediscovery and importation of manuscripts, often artistically and lovingly illustrated after 1250, not only brought great excitement to scholars, but also added a new dimension to life. Manitius lists no manuscripts of Herodotus from the medieval library catalogues. The oldest surviving manuscript of Herodotus is a tenth-century parchment in the Laurentian Library in Florence (*plut.* 70.3). Latin translations often preceded the initial Greek printed editions of the texts. Translations into the vernacular languages quickly followed.[41] Examples of these instruments of a reborn culture may be found in any of the great libraries of Europe. The earliest recorded dictionary was made in 1286 and published in 1460. The Vatican Library has a small lexicon to Herodotus of the fourteenth century,[42] as well as manuscripts of Herodotus of the same general period.[43] The Bibliothèque Nationale in Paris has a manuscript with a vocabulary for Herodotus. Trinity College, Cambridge, has two lexica of Herodotus, of the fifteenth and sixteenth centuries.[44] The Fitzwilliam Museum in Cambridge has manuscripts containing illustrations of both Cyrus and Tomyris. In a manuscript in French of the *Romance of the Rose,* belonging to the fourteenth century, Croesus and Cyrus are brought together in the historic scene of Croesus' rescue from death. Croesus, nude and with bound hands, is led by a rope toward a fire at the base of a column.[45] In another manuscript Croesus is shown hanging nude, crowned, and with bound hands on a wooden gibbet. The executioner is on a ladder.[46]

A manuscript of the fifteenth century in Basel, with German miniatures, illustrates the story of Cyrus twice. The text is that of Nicolaus de Lyra, a commentary on the Bible in the previous century. In one of the miniatures the young Cyrus lies in a crib in swaddling clothes in a forest. He is being suckled by a dog, which has climbed upon the child. His new mother stands beside the crib. The other miniature portrays the discovery of Cyrus by a shepherd.[47]

A manuscript of the fifteenth century in the Fitzwilliam Museum called *Speculum Humanae Salvationis (Mirror of Man's Salvation)* has an illustration of Cyrus in armor lying headless. Tomyris stands there holding her sword and his head.[48] A Renaissance manuscript of Trinity College, Cambridge, cites nine feminine worthies who justify the defense of woman, among them being Tomyris.[49]

Among the Vatican manuscripts is one which contains not only the text of Polyaenus, but also an anonymous work on famous warlike women. Semiramis, Nitocris, and Artemisia are commended. The author cites Ctesias as a source. One suspects that another lady called "Onomaris" (*fol.* 136v.) is, by a corrupt spelling, "Tomyris."[50] The Vatican Library also has Laurentius Valla's partial Latin version of Herodotus, of the middle of the fifteenth century, made, as Valla states, *ut neque ea quae gesta sunt ex rebus humanis obliterentur* (in order that man's accomplishments may not be effaced from human consciousness). This translation went into editions during the remainder of the century. An illuminated parchment copy of this translation, once owned by Lorenzo the Magnificent, is in the Laurentian Library in Florence (*plut.* 67.1). The miniatures are the work of Francesco d'Antonio del Chierico. Part of the initial H on page 1 is a portrait of Herodotus holding a book. Other Latin translations followed, including one by Boiardo, and two editions by Stephanus, the editor of the *Thesaurus Linguae Graecae* (1572), in the sixteenth century. These editions included the fragments of Ctesias. The Walters Art Gallery in Baltimore has a Latin translation of Herodotus of about the year 1500, written in Italy.

The *editio princeps* of Herodotus was the Aldine edition of 1502. The British Museum has a copy of this edition. By 1533 Herodotus had been translated into Italian, by 1535 into German, by 1552 into French, and 1584 into English in the translations of books 1 and 2 by Barnaby Rich. The first complete translation of Herodotus into a modern language was that of Littlebury (1737). Erasmus saw the need of reading Herodotus in the schools. Manuscripts and editions of Xenophon's *Education of Cyrus* also gave fresh impetus to the romantic tradition of Cyrus, which has stimulated interpretation in every age, the latest being Harold Lamb's *Cyrus the Great* in 1960.[51] In the Laurentian Library in Florence there is an edition of Justin's *Epitome*. It was printed in Venice on December 12, 1479. It is the first edition of Justin with an issue date. Through these and many other documents Herodotus in general and the story of Cyrus is particular were vividly presented to a world realizing a new perspective of life.

MACHIAVELLI

In disengaging itself from medieval concepts the Renaissance found it necessary to reappraise the bases of political and social philosophy, and at the same time found at hand in ancient documents a long record of historical writing in which the actions of states and societies were recorded and appraised. The founder of modern political science, fittingly enough, was a man well grounded in ancient history and a student of the Roman historian Livy, namely the Italian Machiavelli (1469–1527). For the solution of problems of political philosophy he, as many who followed him, found it more helpful to return to the experience of the ancient Greeks and Romans than to any body of experience since their time. For during the Middle Ages political science had been superseded by theology. But now, amid the bitter strife of vested interests and ideas in the fifteenth century, Machiavelli was faced with the need for an answer to a problem of military strategy in a setting of political philosophy, namely, whether

one should, when threatened with attack, await the aggressor or mount an offensive. The specifics of his situation are
then further defined, for he assumes that one of the two approximately equal powers has declared war on the other. In
exploring the reasoning of those who felt it better to assume
the offensive against such aggression Machiavelli cites the
advice of Croesus to Cyrus on the borders of the Massagetae
(*Discourses* 2.12.1). Machiavelli knew that Tomyris had given
to Cyrus the choice of entering her territory or of letting her
enter his in setting the field of battle; and that Croesus, contrary to others, had advised Cyrus to seek out his foe. To de-
feat her outside her kingdom would leave her in possession
of it and capable of reforming her troops. Machiavelli notes
that Croesus' advice led to disaster for Cyrus, but in contrast
with Herodotus he fails to identify Cyrus as the aggressor.
Bacon, who had read Machiavelli, raised similar questions of
military strategy and political philosophy in England, and
found an answer in classical mythology.

In his *Art of War* Machiavelli has reversed Herodotus' version of the ruse by which Cyrus defeated part of Tomyris'
army. After mentioning various stratagems by which victory
has been won, such as by exploiting a human propensity to
excessive eating and drinking, by feigning planned retreat,
and by leaving extensive repasts of food and drink, Machiavelli attributes such strategy to Tomyris in her conflict with
Cyrus. Machiavelli could have found textual corroboration
of this version of the story only in the *Stratagems* of the Greek
author Polyaenus, or some derivative of that source. There
was no translation of the text of Polyaenus published before
the death of Machiavelli. Three manuscripts of Polyaenus,
however, were brought to Italy by Michael Apostolius, who
fled from Constantinople and before his death about 1480
copied many manuscripts which found their way into the
libraries of Europe. One of them, from Urbino, is now a part
of the Vatican collection.[52] An Italian translation of Polyaenus
was published a generation after the death of Machiavelli.

BANDELLO

Matteo Bandello (1480–1562) fed an avid hunger in Europe for more complete information about woman than the Middle Ages could provide. The influence of his *Tales (Novelle)* was felt in England within years after his death. One of his *Tales* (3.9) relates the fanciful romance of Cyrus, Panthea, and Abradatas, known through Xenophon's idyllic version in his *Education of Cyrus*. When Cyrus captured Babylon, one of the captives was Panthea, perhaps the most beautiful woman in the Orient. Her husband, Abradatas, a baron under the king of Assyria, was away on a diplomatic mission for his king at the time of the capture of his lovely and devoted wife. Finding Panthea in despair over her plight some barons extended their comfort by greeting her as their future queen, as wife of Cyrus. This thought had also occurred to Cyrus, when he heard of her beauty. But Panthea announced to the barons her resolve to die rather than to submit to such an arrangement. Hearing of her resolve, Cyrus, who was afraid to see Panthea for fear of finding her beauty irresistible, restored the lady to her husband, thereby winning the warm friendship and allegiance of both. In Cyrus' war on Tomyris, queen of the Massagetae, Abradatas was killed. When her husband's body was brought to Panthea, she inflicted on herself a mortal wound and fell over the body of her husband. Bandello in closing his story paid fitting tribute to the eternal fame of her virtue. This rare and incomparable lady both shared her virtues with others and provided an example to them.

Bandello's version of this story differs from that of Xenophon. To the Greek historian Abradatas was the king of Susa. He met his death, according to Xenophon, in Cyrus' campaign against Sardis (546 B.C.). Babylon did not fall to Cyrus until 538 B.C. The captive queen was given into the custody of Araspas for allotment to Cyrus as a prize of war. Because Araspas increasingly forced his attentions upon Panthea, she appealed by letter to Cyrus for protection. This protection

Cyrus gallantly extended to her. Xenophon's account of the last farewell of Panthea and her husband, now a loyal ally of Cyrus, and of the last interview of Abradatas and Cyrus before the former's departure to the most dangerous sector of the front in Cyrus' behalf is both touching and noble. Panthea, on the return of her husband's body, inflicted a mortal wound on herself and in dying laid her head on her husband's bosom.

JOHN MANDEVILLE

The celebrated document which goes under the name of Sir John Mandeville is acquainted with the capture of Babylon by Cyrus. The document seems to have had Continental sources prior to its translation into English.

LYDGATE

John Lydgate (*ca.* 1370–*ca.* 1451), a contemporary and admirer of Chaucer, wrote a long treatise called *Fall of Princes* in English verse in the period 1431–1439. Both the author and his work long enjoyed a popularity which overshadowed—by consensus now, undeservedly—the prestige of Chaucer. Since Lydgate's theme in general is the fall of princes and specifically here the "woful aventure" of Cyrus (2.3731), the early life of Cyrus is passed over with only a brief mention. Cyrus' wolfish thirst for blood made him a tyrant. He grew wanton in robbery and pillage, and his victories brought him much gold. Asia could not content him. He coveted "Cithia," the realm of queen Tomyris, adjoining —if the reader will permit—Ethiopia and India, with the Caucasus on the south. The queen gave one third of her forces to her son, but his innocence led him into the trap set by Cyrus. The son abandoned Mars for Bacchus. Cyrus, returning, killed them all, for there is no resistance in the drunk. But Tomyris repressed the woman in her, and the tears, and vowed revenge. Her simulated fear as she fled into the mountains was the undoing of Cyrus. He was trapped and all of his men were slain. She consigned his head to a bath of blood, and his body to beasts, without benefit of funeral rites. For such a horrible reversal for a great man there is a clear supernatural implication. God and fortune doomed Cyrus' attempt to substitute might for right. Through Tomyris God chastised him (2.3732-3962). For ten stanzas Lydgate reflected on this case history of the divine control of man's ambition.

In the British Museum there is a vellum manuscript, of the middle of the fifteenth century, of Lydgate's *Fall of Princes*. One miniature (Harley 1766,126r.) shows the shepherd Sparagos and his wife holding the infant Cyrus in swaddling clothes in a wooded landscape. They had taken the child from a nursing wolf.[53] The miniature on page 128r. brings Cyrus into the presence of Astyages and soldiers.

LAURENT DE PREMIERFAIT

The two antecedents of the sententious recognition of the precarious nature of high position are, first, Boccaccio's Latin work *De Casibus Virorum et Feminarum Illustrium* and, second, an amplified French prose version entitled *Des cas des nobles hommes et femmes* of Laurent de Premierfait, who died in the early fifteenth century. Laurent likewise made French translations of Cicero's two golden essays on old age and friendship. His knowledge of Latin served him well in this important work of disseminating ancient culture and thereby re-educating Europe. A half page of Boccaccio sometimes appears as several columns in the text of Laurent.

In the British Museum there is a vellum manuscript of the end of the fifteenth century containing a French translation of Boccaccio's *De Casibus* by Laurent de Premierfait, and illustrated with miniatures, some of which are in the style of Jehan Foucquet. The miniature on page 54v. shows Astyages arranging to serve to Harpagus, his guest, the son of Harpagus on a platter. In this miniature Mandane also appears, and Cyrus being suckled by a dog.[54]

GOLDING

Golding's translation of Justin, which appeared in 1570, gave further circulation to Justin's version of the story of Cyrus.

PETTIE

John Pettie's *Petite Pallace of Pleasure* (1576) was a collection of stories in prose written about and for women. In his story of St. Alexius, who abandoned marriage and spent the rest of his life in making pilgrimages, he comments on the stout courage of woman, and cites Tomyris, slayer of the mighty Cyrus, as an example.

SHAKESPEARE

Tomyris was part of the well-stocked mind of Shakespeare. In the first part of *Henry VI* (2.3.5-6) the Countess of Auvergne in plotting the death of Talbot says:

> I shall as famous be by this exploit
> As Scythian Tomyris by Cyrus' death.

Later she calls Talbot a shrimp (2.3.23) and a bloodthirsty lord (2.3.34).

PAINTING

The well-established place of Cyrus' tragic fate in literature insured him at least a modest place in the ideology of painting. Cyrus was a useful subject for dramatic narrative, as well as an example in the code of morality, which painting served. Kings, on the other hand, might well prefer some more pleasant return on their investment than the kind of death which the narrative of Herodotus or Dante portrayed for the Persian king.

A fine fresco of Tomyris by the early Florentine Andrea dal Castagno (1390–1457) has been recovered from oblivion and is now in the Castagno Museum in S. Apollonia in Florence. The fresco is one of a series of heroes and heroines set in rec-

tangular niches by pilasters. The early Renaissance empha-
sized fame and glory as within life's dimensions. It selected its
examples with a discriminating catholicity. In the series are
statesmen, generals, and poets, all from the late Middle Ages
or early Renaissance. The poets honored were Dante,
Petrarch, and Boccaccio. The three heroines, Esther, the
Cumaean Sibyl, and Tomyris, are all from ancient lore, pagan
or biblical. The animation of the figures suggests either conversation among them or an awareness of spectators. Tomyris
is a graceful, striking young queen. Under her long tunic she
wears armor. Her raised right hand rests on the butt of a
spear. A plait of hair falls down over her right shoulder. On
her head she wears a jewel-studded crown. She coyly raises
her robe on the left side, exposing her ankle.[55]

A *cassone* in the British Museum portrays Cyrus in the
probably unhistorical act of beheading the son of Tomyris,
and the revenge of the mother.[56]

One of the finest examples of Rubens' talent in an English
private collection is his *Thomyris and Cyrus* in the collection
of Lord Darnley. Amid an attentive group of women on the
left and of men on the right an attendant at the bidding of his
queen lowers the head of Cyrus into a jar of blood. A few
years later Rubens made another version of this gruesome act
in a painting now in the Louvre. In a group of men and
women, Tomyris, sitting on a throne, watches her order
being carried out.[57] A copy of this version made by Nicolas de
Largillierre (1656–1746) is in the Museum of Toulouse.[58]

The French painter Collin de Vermont (1693–1761) identified himself with the classical tradition during his sojourn of
five years in Rome. His series of 32 pictures on the history of
Cyrus is a complete biography of the Persian king, from the
prophesy of his birth by Isaiah to the homage rendered to him
by Alexander the Great at his tomb. In one painting Harpagus receives the head of his son. The romance of Panthea and
Abradatas is also represented. Another painting in this series
presents the immersion of Cyrus' head in a pot of blood. The

paintings were made around the middle of the eighteenth century, and represent the best work of the painter. The collection is now dispersed.[59]

TAPESTRY

That there was a general reawakening in Europe in the twelfth century one can see in the development of the weaving industry from a minor trade into an international instrument of culture. Illustrative expression in the manual skills found a high degree of articulateness in the vision, eloquence, and excitement of literature. Materials had also to be at hand, as well as a widespread need for a finished product, and the ability to market the product. It was now men's slow task to recover a complex social life and a universal human perspective. During the twelfth century the wool supplied by the Cistercian monasteries in Northumberland found its way to Flemish towns, where it was processed into textiles. And in northern Europe a demand was at hand for cloth for both ornament and warmth. Thanks to the weaving industry and the sale of its products the Flemish towns of Arras, Bruges, Ghent, and Ypres prospered and grew.

The Crusades (1095–1291) were also an important force in the economic, social, and cultural revival of Europe. The goods of the Levant and the Far East, among them always silk, wool, cotton, and dyes, found ready markets through Europe via Sicily, the cities of Lombardy, Bapaume in France, and intinerant Catalan merchants. The greatest of the fairs of Europe was that at Champagne to the east of Paris.

As Arras declined after the middle of the fifteenth century, Brussels began a long period of unprecedented prosperity in weaving. Many centers of weaving also brought prosperity to France, Germany, Italy, Spain, England, and Ireland. From the early thirteenth century Florence surpassed her neighbors as a producer of cloth and as a center for commerce and banking. In 1546 a manufactory was founded at Florence under the patronage of Cosimo I. The still famous Gobelins' manufactory in Paris was established in 1662 by order of Louis XIV; and in 1720 Philip V of Spain brought Jacques van der Goten from Antwerp to establish in Madrid the Royal Tapestry Factory, still in operation today.

Dozens of other manufactories of tapestry contributed to the prosperity of Medieval and Renaissance Europe. Hands were kept busy, and verdant pasture lands were happy to co-operate in supplying the raw material. Work passed into skill, trade, and fine art, and found enriching associations with other arts, especially literature and painting. The skills of the tapestry weavers enriched not only their pocketbooks, but their minds and spirits. In creating and selling their fine products far and wide across the otherwise segregating frontiers men lifted themselves and Europe into a culture in which the best of the past had an important civilizing effect. Wool, silks, and dyes—the basic ingredients of the craft—have the further comfort that they do not explode.

The tapestry weavers went to the ancient experience because, as they had learned in the schools, in literature, and in the sister art of painting, it represented—to speak figuratively—the best keyboard available by which the total melody of life could be realized. Legend, history, and religion, mostly from the remote past, provided wholesome and inspiring contacts of the present with the past. Through the legendary mist with which the *cursus vitae* of Cyrus soon embellished itself there are clear indications of nobility and magnanimity. Xenophon in his *Education of Cyrus* also made of Cyrus' career a politically and historically distorting romantic novel, and the influence of this charming work in the history of tapestry is as easy to trace as it is delightful to see. The culture of Europe in the Renaissance was oriented to the nobility. In their endeavor to see themselves in the best light the nobles found the legends and early history of Greece and Rome an unusually flattering mirror, just as did the Greeks and Romans who transmitted these legends into the stream of Western culture.

Some tapestries depicting Cyrus are based partly on a document relating the heroic deeds of Cyrus composed by the Count of Lucena in 1470.[60] The revenge and retribution represented by Tomyris and presented in the work of Boccaccio and of the translation of it by Laurent de Premierfait were also often depicted. The channels by which a knowledge of Cyrus reached the West have already been discussed. It was not necessary that a knowledge of him await the *editio princeps* of Herodotus in 1502 or of Xenophon's works in 1516.

The Gardner Museum in Boston has a set of five tapestries woven in Brussels in the second quarter of the sixteenth century. The set once belonged to the Barberini family in Rome. All five tapestries depict scenes from the life of Cyrus, as follows:

1) Astyages directs Harpagus to dispose of the infant Cyrus.

2) A messenger from Harpagus brings to Cyrus a letter concealed in a hare.

3) Harpagus is appointed commander of an army by the king. Whether the king is Astyages or Cyrus is not clear.

4) Tomyris receives the messenger who bears a proposal of wedlock from Cyrus.

5) Tomyris learns that her son has been captured by Cyrus. The revenge of Tomyris on Cyrus does not survive as part of the series.[61]

Records show that a weaving of the history of Cyrus was made in the manufactory of Florence in 1566, established 20 years earlier by Cosimo I, and that it produced on a large scale.

Two wonderful series of tapestries on the history of Cyrus found their way to Madrid. They were made either in Brussels or by artists from Brussels. Of the 14 original pieces of one series 10 survive, the work of the skilled Johann van Tiegen for Count Wilhelm von Hessen-Kassel shortly after the middle of the sixteenth century. The loving care with which they were made is evident in their workmanship. The other series was woven probably by Nicolas Leiniers.[62] One of these tapestries shows Cyrus extending mercy to Croesus, with details of the fall of Sardis in the background. An inscription woven into the top of the tapestry recalls the celebrated passage of Herodotus (1.86) in which Croesus, about to be burned alive on a funeral pyre by order of Cyrus, recalled the words of Solon that no man while living is blest, thereby winning the pity of Cyrus:

> Croesus, rogo impositus, fit memor dicti Solonis, quo Cirus admonitus, vicissitudine rerum perpensa, Croesum cum coeteris iubet deponi.[63]

> Croesus, placed on the pyre, remembers the statement of Solon, by which Cyrus, having been admonished and having weighed the capriciousness of human affairs, orders Croesus and the others to be taken down.

The West had kept alive the tradition of Croesus through the Middle Ages, as it had of other personages prominent in the pages of Herodotus, but after the middle of the fifteenth century the text of Herodotus was available directly through the Latin translation of Laurentius Valla.

Among other pieces of the series was a scene of the childhood of Cyrus, another of the recognition of the young Cyrus by Astyages, and another of the capture of Astyages by Cyrus. The struggle of Cyrus with Croesus is also represented, as well as the reception of a messenger of Tomyris by Cyrus, and the sadistic immersion of Cyrus' head in a blood bath.

In the middle of the seventeenth century a quasi-historical novel by Mlle. Madeleine Scudéry brought a kind of Frenchified Cyrus into tapestry. The novel, in ten volumes, was entitled *Artamène or Cyrus the Great (Artamène ou le grand Cyrus)*. Mlle. Scudéry (1607–1701), the incomparable Sappho of her day, through her novels and her charming salon was the delight of France and of Europe. In the fabric of her novel and of the tapestries inspired by it one may see the ideal romantic hero, a splendid, perfumed, feathered grand signor in whom any French king would be flattered to see his image. The novel is replete with conversation, incidents, and crises with happy endings. Cyrus is the grandson of Astyages. He saw, loved, and wooed the lovely Mandane, daughter of the Cappadocian Cyaxares, after first seeing her in her royal retinue. The abduction of Mandane for the evil king of the Assyrians drove Cyrus to furious revenge. Mandane, coveted by many, was finally brought to the protection of Croesus, to his sorrow, for he was to fall under the power of Cyrus. As a further complication, Mandane fell into the hands of Aryante, the brother of Queen Tomyris. The Queen, inflamed with a hopeless love for Cyrus, sought out her rival Mandane with hostile intent. When Cyrus too was taken captive, Tomyris decided to stab the two lovers. But Cyrus managed to disarm the guard of the prison. After escaping he wrought a horrible blood bath on the Massagetae. Tomyris fled in terror. Cyrus and Mandane were then wedded with fitting splendor.[64]

Around the middle of the seventeenth century the French master Jean Boffinet in the celebrated weaving center of Aubusson supplied for Count Antoine de La Rocheaymon a series of tapestries on Cyrus which were based on Mlle. Scudéry's novel.[65] Tapestries on the history of Cyrus and on Cyrus and Mandane are known to have been made in France around the last half of the seventeenth century.[66] The Benjamin Franklin Hotel in Philadelphia has a series of tapestries on the story of Cyrus, from the seventeenth century. Other tapestries of the same nature are in private collections in America.[67]

In 1669 the Brussels weaver Erasmus de Pannemaker contracted to supply a series of six tapestries on the history of Cyrus.[68] Surviving account books from Antwerp show that a very popular incident in the history of Cyrus for portrayal on tapestries was the presentation of Panthea to Cyrus, a fine tribute to the vitality of this romantic episode found in the *Education of Cyrus* by Xenophon.[69]

A tapestry portraying the childhood of Cyrus was manufactured at Santa Bárbara in Madrid about 1745, and is still in that city.[70] The signature of Jacobo van der Goten confirms the Dutch origin of the Spanish Royal Factory. This tapestry shows Cyrus as a baby being entrusted to a shepherd and reared in a tent amid a paradise of forests, flowers, and wild and domesticated animals. But the buildings in the dim background indicate that royal quarters are not far away. The Latin inscription at the top of the tapestry is not completely legible in the available illustration. A plaque in the lower right-hand corner bears the legend:

Regnum autem iustitia et liberalitate.

Sovereign power under justice and freedom.

The political ideal corresponds with the romantic tradition attached to the name of Cyrus, and the noble owners of this tapestry would also like to enjoy a vicarious association with the ideal.

In the early eighteenth century the manufactory of Jakob van Zeunen in Brussels supplied a set of large tapestries portraying the life of Cyrus for the splendid palace of Johann Keyssler in Turin.[71] In this city, too, Charles Emmanuel III established a manufactory for Demignot of the Florence shop. By the middle of the eighteenth century the manufactory had produced 34 pieces, among them portrayals of the history of Cyrus.

Jacobo van der Goten of Antwerp, requested by Philip V of Spain to establish the Royal Tapestry Factory in Madrid in 1720, began his work there by copying old sets of tapestries, among them the story of Cyrus.[72]

REVIEW

Cyrus the Great was a history-maker born into a myth-making age. The myth-makers soon clothed him for a role which began with romance, crested in epic, and hurried along into tragedy. There were those who claimed to know the real

Cyrus without benefit of high boot and purple robe, but the passion of the play needed a subject capable of living nobly, of bearing a tragic flaw, and eventually of succumbing to it in the grand style. The myth-makers have had their way. The Cyrus of history, like the Hamlet of history, is overshadowed by his own image projected upon a backdrop revealing a divine plan and control of human ambition.

Ctesias wanted to break the tragic mold in which Herodotus had cast Cyrus and Astyages. For his stage he wanted more subdued lights, less stately robes, and a more secular backdrop. Cyrus was born without incident, led a normal life of Oriental intrigue, and, as usually happens, was killed by his intended victims, the Dubikes (whoever they were).

Xenophon, on the other hand, in his narrative, found a home for his political and social reflections not in some anonymous person still to be born, but in an already known and manifestly noble historical figure who could still bear the play of fanciful imagination.

In the Roman world the tradition of Cyrus lived through various derivative sources originating directly or indirectly in the previously mentioned Greek sources, which, as we have seen, failed to find a uniform basis of fact regarding Cyrus. Some of these authors in the Roman world wrote in Greek and others in Latin. Their interests vary, ranging over the fields of history, geography, didactic anecdotes, military strategy, rhetoric, and satire.

Though some of the Christian fathers who followed these sources of the Roman world were still able to read Greek documents, the Roman writers of the Middle Ages depended on Latin sources for their information. Had it not been for the record of Cyrus preserved in the Roman sources in the West, both the name of Herodotus and the content of his *History* would have been lost for many centuries. As it was, even the Latin sources which kept alive the content of parts of Herodotus' *History* often failed to associate his name with it. St. Ambrose saw in Cyrus an example of the folly of pride. St.

Jerome, on the other hand, in his references to Cyrus, shows himself not so much a moralist as a scholar. He shared Josephus' reverence for this friend of the Jews. The influence of Josephus' regard for Cyrus lingered on through many centuries.

The medieval writers often follow known Roman sources closely, with Orosius and Petrus Comestor depending on Justin, and Jordanes depending on Cassiodorus. One of the oldest functions of history is the moral one of preserving a record of the virtues, and instilling in future generations a fear of base words and deeds for the bad name associated with them. So wrote Tacitus in the first century:

> Praecipuum munus annalium reor ne virtutes sileantur, utque pravis dictis factisque ex posteritate et infamia metus sit (*Annals* 3.65).

> I regard it as the special responsibility of records that virtues should not be reduced to silence, and that ignoble words and deeds should inspire fear for their bad repute in years to come.

Dante wedded this kind of didactic history to literature. The pageant of history, he felt, made manifest the working of God's will. Petrarch saw in heroic people of the past the dynamism of triumphant virtue. Boccaccio looked upon history as proof of the vanity of human ambition in a divinely controlled world. Cyrus became an object lesson of the futility of covetous ambition. The influence of Boccaccio was widespread. The *Gesta Romanorum* saw in Cyrus' stratagem against the army of Tomyris a warning against the evils of "drink." Through Christine de Pisan Christian morality attended the story of Cyrus into France and England.

In the Renaissance Machiavelli searched anew amid ancient experience, especially Roman, for expedient procedure by which one might survive one's foe. Thus a basis for political science other than in classical ethics was established, and governments since that time have barely subscribed to any-

thing better than their own best interests, often narrowly in-
terpreted. Bandello gave both man and woman a chance to
demonstrate a preference for nobility and chastity even unto
death, though the chance of war gave to those concerned the
choice of taking the spoils traditionally belonging to the
victor. Xenophon's *Education of Cyrus* had a social environment in which it might enjoy a popularity and mold a culture
to a degree hitherto unknown.

From the early Renaissance the art of painting gave a new
vividness to the story of Cyrus, and undoubtedly introduced
the story to many who would not, or could not, have been
influenced by it in literature. The miniaturist Jehan Foucquet,
as one example among many, applied his craft to manuscripts,
lifting them to a high level of beauty and vividness, and
through his art he carried the culture of ancient Rome into
his native France. The sister art of tapestry also gave to the
story of Cyrus a chance to infiltrate into the consciousness of
craftsmen and tradesmen all over Europe. The indebtedness
of tapestry and the other manual arts to literature is seen in
the influence of the novel of Mlle. Scudéry on the manual
arts; and, in turn, the economics of the weaving trade gave
to the early origins of the Greek experience a chance to carry
a renascent culture to honorable prosperity.

The Renaissance inherited from the Middle Ages the documents pertaining to Cyrus which had long lain dormant. The
recovery of these documents, coinciding roughly with the invention of printing, was soon followed by published translations and texts. A new and better perspective of life imple-
mented by instruments leading to trades, crafts, and fine arts
was opened by them. The course of history and the place of
personalities in it became more clear. But for the Renaissance
and subsequent times it was impossible, even with these
newly found documents, in casting aside the misconceptions
of the Middle Ages, to arrive at what may be called historical
truth. For already among those who constitute our earliest
historical sources important material facts were in dispute.

Such a base of facts had to be assumed; and the nature of the base differed among the assumers. From this point history consists in an ethical or theological context superimposed on assumptions. The context may be the personal point of view of the writer, or it may be of a whole society of people committed to a point of view. The point of view may include or exclude the functioning of the divine in human affairs. In reality the reaction of a reflective Greek and Roman society to the commonly accepted tradition of Cyrus' death varied little from the Christian reaction. Christian humanism was the child of pagan humanism. Therefore the recovery in the Renaissance of the documents of the pagan tradition of Cyrus brought not a sharp break in the tradition of Cyrus, but rather a confirmation of the tradition, with a clearer historical perspective in time. As future periods ceased to subscribe to the point of view to which the tradition of Cyrus lent itself in the ancient and medieval world, and became engrossed in other points of view, Cyrus ceases to be an educating force in society, but remains an interesting part of an historical record. But the fact remains that through most of Western culture, in one way or another, Cyrus the Great has been an educating force either as warning or as ideal.

The Story of Lucretia

LIVY

The first version of the story of Lucretia told with imaginative skill in Latin is found in Livy's *History of Rome* (1.57-60), composed around the beginning of the Christian era a half millennium after the event is reported to have happened. Cicero's brief references to the story (*Republic* 2.25.46 and *De Finibus* 2.20.66) are not to be compared in literary quality with Livy's version.

The Rutulian town of Ardea, some 20 miles south of Rome, had been placed under siege by the Etruscan king, Tarquin the Proud. During a carousal of the young nobles in the Roman encampment the conversation turned to their wives. As the young men warmed up to their subject, each one extolling his own wife, Collatinus of Collatia (a town of Latium) suggested that the preeminence of his wife Lucretia could be established in a matter of hours by an unheralded visit to their homes. Flushed with wine, the young men all agreed to the proposal, and took to their horses. At Rome they found their wives reveling even while the first shades of evening were falling; whereas at Collatia they found Lucretia spinning and weaving by lamplight with her handmaids. Conceded victory, Collatinus extended hospitality to his companions. Before they returned to camp, Sextus Tarquin, the son of Tarquin the Proud and kinsman of Collatinus, fired by the beauty and chastity of Lucretia, had conceived a lustful passion to possess her.

After a few days Sextus made a secret visit to Collatia. As a kinsman he was cordially received, dined, and offered shelter for the night. In the still of the night, with drawn sword, he sought Lucretia's bedroom. Catching her by surprise, he told her who he was, that he was armed, and that at the risk of her life she should stay quiet. During her first paralyzed fright he tried every tactic by which the will of a woman could be moved—but to no avail. But though death could not influence her, the threat of dishonor did. For he threatened to kill her, and to place beside her the nude body of a slave, and then to claim that by the right sanctioned by their society he had slain both of them when caught in adultery. The ruse succeeded.

In the morning Lucretia sadly sent off an identical message to her father and husband, asking them to come at once to learn of a terrible atrocity. They and their companions, P. Valerius and L. Junius Brutus, found her sitting disconsolate in her bedroom. A flood of tears preceded her story. She regarded the loss of honor in a woman to be the supreme loss. Until the end of the Renaissance, in every retelling of the story, she was urged to maintain her attitude by men who held no such self-imposed restriction. But first she established—before death as her witness—that while her body was violated, she was innocent in intent. She wanted not only to *be* chaste, but to *be known to be* chaste. She named the adulterer, and exacted of her kinsmen a solemn pledge to seek revenge on one who had used the code of hospitality as a means of violating her. In Latin a *hospes* (guest) had become a *hostis* (public enemy). Giving their pledge forthwith, they comforted the distraught lady with the assurance that compulsion had legally absolved her of any guilt. Reminding the men of the responsibility devolving upon them, she absolved herself of guilt, but not of punishment. No immodest woman, she reasoned, in years to come shall live under a precedent of extenuating circumstances to excuse her guilt. So, plunging a knife to her heart, Lucretia fell over dead.

Livy then relates the train of events set in motion by the violation and death of Lucretia, which led soon to the expulsion of Tarquin the Proud to Caere and of Sextus to Gabii, where he was soon assassinated. With the election of the first two consuls, Brutus and Collatinus, the Roman Republic was born.

The story of Lucretia came to Livy from the annalists of the third and second centuries B.C. It was concerned with a Roman lady who held herself to an absolute standard of chastity, as then expected by society and sanctioned by law. The story contained elements—found also in other stories of world literature—which have often fed but rarely satisfied the hunger of Western society, however simple or developed, however fresh or jaded the appetite. The wager over the fairest lady, the provocativeness of feminine chastity, seduction by a kinsman, violated hospitality, slandered chastity, and the exploitation of women by those in power—constituent parts of the story related by Livy with admirable conciseness—find their counterparts in other stories of world literature.[1]

ROME'S HEROIC PERIOD

Lucretia is but one of the many heroic figures of Rome's formative period. The composite of those men and women presents a consistent picture of heroism, self-sacrifice, civic responsibility, integrity, humility, and solemn dignity such as have never been given to any other nation to exemplify so clearly. The specific names which rise from the society, as sparks which represent the fire, are—to name but a few—Collatinus, Brutus, Horatius, Cloelia, Cincinnatus, Titus Manlius, and P. Decius Mus and his descendants. Echoes of their sterling qualities vibrated down through the bare annals of early Roman history until a time when Livy could eloquently pay them their due tribute.

The age of Livy, Vergil, Horace, and of Augustus, after whom it was named, grew into full stature in the image of the early builders of Roman society. With the Augustans a century of indecision and abandonment of national heritage had ended. The example of the forefathers gave clear guidance to a fallen society in the fulfillment of a new destiny. The *mores* of the early seven hills formed the solid base of human integrity and dignity on which Rome could now govern the world in "virtue, clemency, justice, and piety," as Augustus expressed it in his last will and testament, the Monument of Ancyra. In the preface to his *History* Livy admonished each reader to give strict attention to the life, the *mores,* the men, and the arts by which the empire had been acquired and grew. Both Horace and Vergil also gave noble expression to this romantic idealization of Rome's heroic period. One facet of the old image was the story of Lucretia. Long after that time the West found this story a guiding light in its social growth.

ATTITUDES TOWARD ADULTERY

The violation of Lucretia posed for Roman jurists a nice legal problem, and for her a personal ethical problem. Dionysius of Halicarnassus (2.25.1-7) states the legal process by which Lucretia would be judged. It should be noted that it is the woman who will be judged, and who must pay the penalty. Sextus will be punished by revolutionary, extra-legal methods. Dionysius attributed to Romulus in the eighth century a law designed to insure chastity and propriety in women. Certain improprieties placed a woman at the legal mercy of the injured party. Other more serious offenses, however, such as adultery and the drinking of wine—regarded as the forerunner of adultery—placed a woman in the hands of her male relatives and her husband. Death was a permissible penalty for these gravest of offenses by a woman. Dionysius observes that both of these offenses were long treated by the Romans with ruthless severity. He felt that the length of time during which the law was enforced was an index of its wisdom. As a matter of historical fact, legislation which gathered around certain names and dates in early Roman history arose, in all likelihood, from the gradual hardening of social point of view and judicial practice into law. But there can be no doubt that the story of Lucretia proves the attitude of merciless severity in early Rome toward licentiousness in women.

The shame of dishonor with which Sextus threatened Lucretia—a shame which she would be unable to refute if slain —made her an inevitable victim of his lust. The penalty of death was permissible, but not mandatory. The humane provision of the law, which was immediately extended by the father and the husband, Lucretia might, under the circumstances, have safely assumed. Livy's version contains this element of humaneness in the interpretation of the law.[2] The Laws of the Twelve Tables also reveal not only the primitive severity of an early day, but also the humaneness of a later version. In order, however, to avoid setting a precedent for other women less severe in their moral standards Lucretia preferred, after having established her innocence, to impose upon herself the penalty of death. No one questioned her right to do so, although the deed was an act of injustice to herself and although the justice of lenience was immediately pointed out to her by her male kinsmen.

Adultery and the forcible seizure of women carry one not only into severity, as in early Rome, but into irrational superstitions among less enlightened and more primitive peoples. Adultery was thought to bring the anger of the divine upon a community, sometimes in the form of a failure of the crops, or of some other disturbance of the course of nature. Sometimes in the East Indies it was thought to bring on a plague of tigers, or crocodiles, or heavy rains. It was punished in the most fantastic ways: by burial alive for both parties, by roasting of the adulterer, by strangulation and casting into a river, by drowning, and by flaying alive and eating.[3]

LUCRETIA AND ANTIGONE

The story of the Roman heroine Lucretia may be compared and contrasted with Sophocles' *Antigone* (441 B.C.). In that tragedy Antigone, in violation of royal decree, performed for the body of her brother the ceremonial rites of burial, thereby incurring the penalty of death. She claimed the priority over

the royal decree of the obligation of sister to brother as a
higher law binding the human and the divine. Creon, king of
Thebes, not recognizing the claim, imposed the final penalty
upon Antigone, even though she was to be his own daughter-
in-law through marriage with his son Haemon. But in her
Roman story Lucretia, the defendant, took the law into her
own hands. The higher and humane interpretation of the law
was placed upon it by her male kinsmen. In both stories death
came to the heroine: in the *Antigone* because Creon's change
of heart came too late, for both Antigone and her fiancé had
committed suicide; and in the other because Lucretia took
her life before she could be restrained. The two stories are
representative of their respective cultures. Antigone's asser-
tion of the preeminence of certain inalienable human rights
—in defense of the individual against arbitrary decree—is in-
dicative of the central humanity of Athenian culture at its
best; Lucretia, on the other hand, symbolizes an acute sense
of civic responsibility of the individual to society, in which
even injustice to the one might eventually redound to the
benefit of the other.

DIODORUS

Diodorus of Sicily, a compiler of historical events who
wrote a *Library of History* in Greek a generation before
Christ, inserts one paragraph (20) into his tenth book regarding the violation of Lucretia by Sextus Tarquin. The most obvious traits of his version of the story are his lack of imagination and his literalness. The bare details of his story, though
not his language, coincide partly with the version of his contemporary Dionysius of Halicarnassus. While availing himself
of the hospitality of Lucretia's absent husband, Sextus appeared at her door in the night, sword in hand, and with no
recorded motivation other than his obvious motive, and he
announced his plan to slay her and implicate her with a dead
slave if she did not submit. But if she would submit, he
promised to make her his wife. He did not say how this

could be done, and the Rome of the time did not condone
polygamy. The three qualities of Lucretia, rapidly noted,
are her beauty, chastity, and fear. In the morning she summoned her kinsmen, asked for revenge, and forestalled any
replies by committing suicide. Some details mentioned by
Dionysius, who was Diodorus' contemporary, are omitted.
Facts are facts; motivations are extrinsic. This is a chronicle,
not a history.

The text of Diodorus in chapter 21 turns to a formal en-
comium of Lucretia for the nobility of her decision and for
the effect it should have on others when involved, however
innocently, in unlawful acts. In the light of the dryness of
Diodorus in such matters, editors suspect Byzantine con-
tamination of the text. The political repercussions which
attended the violation of Lucretia are not included in the
surviving fragments of the text of Diodorus.

DIONYSIUS OF HALICARNASSUS

Dionysius of Halicarnassus composed his *Roman Antiquities* in Rome, his adopted home, but in his native language,
Greek, in the generation before the Christian era. He was,
therefore, contemporary with the best years of Vergil,
Horace, and Livy in Rome. He asked history to bear both
morality and eloquence. His work is not without historical
value, since, as he indicates in dealing with Lucretia (4.64.3),
he had consulted "Fabius and the other historians." Q. Fabius
Pictor is an important historical source in Greek of the third
century B.C. His work survives only in fragmentary form.
There are identical features, but also variations, in the contemporary versions of Dionysius, Livy, and Ovid. The third
century sources, if identical, must have been bare of detail.
But later historians were quick to remedy this defect. The
visit of Sextus to Collatia, in the version of Dionysius, came
not from gossip around a campfire, but in the course of offi-
cial business, and since Lucretia's husband happened to be
at camp at the time, Sextus had the chance to seduce her,

which he had long wanted to do. The emotional tone of the account is flat and pedestrian. Ovid, had he read the page which related the violation, must have thought Lucretia an uninteresting victim and the assailant an artless lover. She awakened to find him menacing her with sword and threats. Ovid's *Art of Love,* to be written later, shows that there were more gracious ways to the heart of a lady than this "tough" approach.

Sextus promised to make Lucretia his wife and his queen; for good measure more distant realms were promised. He prevailed over her by using the threat of implicating her with a dead slave. Lucretia is characterized with only three words: beauty, chastity, and fear. No further psychological elaboration is given. On the next morning she rode clad in black raiment to her father's house in Rome, and soon unburdened herself of her misfortune. Having begged for revenge, but before having received any absolution of guilt, she took her life. Her husband arrived too late. History is at times authentic in its lack of artistic form.

In the version of Dionysius (4.82.3) Brutus attributes the suicide of Lucretia to her desire to avoid a similar indignity in the future; whereas in Livy's version (1.58.10) Lucretia refuses to consider herself absolved of punishment, nor will she, however innocent, set an example for another less innocent woman at a later time. Dionysius states (4.82.3) that Lucretia, though a woman, has the resolution of a man. Ovid, though recognizing the same contrast (*animi matrona virilis, Fasti* 2.847), took pains to show that her very innocence gave her a feminine seductiveness. A comparison of the two versions of Dionysius and Livy leaves no doubt that the stern Paduan has written in shorter space a more dramatic and a better motivated and organized story, and possibly at the same time a less historical record. In the versions of Livy and Ovid, Lucretia summoned her father and husband to Collatia. Both Dionysius and Livy state that Collatinus happened to be coming to Rome from camp when the report of foul play reached him. Ovid, too, like Dionysius, clothed Lucretia in black, "as a mother preparing to go to the funeral of a son" (*Fasti* 2.814). Dionysius needed but four paragraphs (4.64-67) for this part of his story. The development of the political repercussions under the guidance of Brutus, however, required 18 additional paragraphs (4.68-85) in which the author's oratorical skill and interest in constitutional theory and procedures are vested in the society of Rome in the sixth century B.C. As early as the fourth century the Greek annalist Ephorus observed that profuse details regarding remote events justify suspicion of the validity of both.

OVID

In the second book of the *Fasti* (721–852), an imaginative and sympathetic account of Rome's festivals, Ovid related the story which led to the expulsion of the dynasty of Tarquins from Rome. He and Livy have an identical content in their two versions, and an occasional similarity in vocabulary.[4] The differences, however, are those of the two personalities, and are as far apart as are didactic idealism in prose and tongue-in-cheek eroticism in verse. The two versions are of approximately equal length, but whereas Livy gives about 75 lines to the violation of Lucretia and nearly the same number to its political repercussions, Ovid, on the other hand, gives over 100 lines to the violation and only 15 lines to the repercussions. Moreover, Ovid's distinctive contribution lies in the former rather than in the latter.

Livy tells his story in a context of early puritanical Rome. An understandable carousal among young men in camp led to a casual reference to women. The beauty and exciting chastity of Lucretia are but mentioned. Ovid, however, notes at greater length not only her manifestations of complete devotion: in her late hours at the loom, the prayer, the fear, the tears, the despondency, and the embrace of complete abandonment at their reunion, but also the catastrophic effect of all this on Sextus Tarquin, who observed it. Sextus noted also her beauty, her snow-white complexion and blond hair, her unaffected good taste, her words, tone, and irreproachable modesty. Absence brought him delightful visions of her posture, her dress, and her skill. The casual fall of the locks upon her neck, and again her features, her words, complexion, appearance, and beautiful face distracted him in a way which prompted an epic comparison with wind and sea. The outcome of an attempted assault was doubtful, but with force, guile, and bravado the risk was worth taking. One would think that Sextus must have read Ovid's *Art of Love,* at least the first book of it, which would have told him that not bashfulness, but bravado won the nod of Luck and Venus:

> Fuge, rustice, longe
> hinc, pudor! Audentem Forsque Venusque iuvat (1.607f.),

> Away from here, countrified modesty!
> It is the bold that Lady Luck and Venus help.

and, with a slight modification, this soldier of fortune went down into the lists of love with a motto for his standard:

> Audentes forsque deusque iuvat (*Fasti* 2.782).

> 'Tis those who are bold that luck and god help.

The fact that Gabii had succumbed to the same technique on his part (*vi, . . . fraude ac dolo,* Livy 1.53.4) encouraged him. Again a liberal education had justified itself by its practicality, for had not Ovid in the *Amores* (1.9.1) pointed out that every lover is a soldier—*Militat omnis amans?*

In the awakening of Lucretia by the intruder Ovid stays close enough to Livy to keep his story within the bounds of history, and he expands the liveliness of Livy with colloquialism and direct quotation; but the feminist and wit in him overcome any part of him which may have been historian. The surprise was total (*Illa nihil,* 2.797). Ovid was right, Sextus must have thought, when he wrote in the *Amores* (1.9.21)

Saepe soporatos invadere profuit hostes.

It has often proved profitable to attack the foe when
deep in slumber.

She had no voice, nor power of speech or mind. But when one
trembles in verse, a comparison is expected. She was like a
young lamb beneath a deadly wolf (2.800). But when thought
finally comes, it should be revealed. Resist? Both history and
instinct tell her that resistance is an incentive to conquest.
Shout? This is to invite death. Run? But how, when he holds
her as he does? The enemy-lover *(amans hostis)* plies her—
did not Livy say so—with entreaties and threats, but the
worldly-wise Ovid prompted the lover to try a fee too! Lucretia succumbed quickly under the same guile as in Livy,
and both writers comment on the emptiness of the lover's
success.

By this time the spirit of the *Art of Love* has vanished, and
Ovid reverts to the original historical context of the story.
In both versions the father and husband agreed that the use
of force insured the innocence of Lucretia, but Ovid does not
further explore the legal phase of the situation. Lucretia
quickly exacted of herself the supreme penalty. Ovid attributed to her last moment the desire not to fall indecorously.
In closing the rest of the story within a few lines he pays dignified tribute to this matron with the courage of a man, whose
body, borne to its last rites, drew with it the tears and resentment of its attendants:

Fertur in exequias animi matrona virilis
et secum lacrimas invidiamque trahit (2.847f.).

This lady of manly spirit is borne to her last rites
and draws with her tears and hatred.

Animi matrona virilis is Ovid's answer to the deprecation
carried in Sextus' estimation of his victim connoted by *mulie-
brem animum* (Livy 1.58.3).

Thus in these two versions of the same story by contemporary writers each reveals his own personality. Ovid wrote his never-completed *Fasti* in the first decade of the Christian era, and his *Art of Love* a few years earlier.

This romantic and tragic portrayal of a sixth-century Roman matron is a providential anticipation of man's concept of the ideal woman at the end of the Renaissance. For the image of the complete woman by that time revealed the qualities of chastity, purity of mind, modesty, humility, constancy and temperance, piety, and the outer manifestations of humanity, courtesy, hospitality, courage, justice, prudence, and learning.[5]

Thus the ancient tradition of independent and enlightened womanhood provided a matrix for a new flowering in the Renaissance. Ovid instructed and delighted the centuries following him. The eleventh and twelfth centuries witnessed a veritable *aetas Ovidiana*. A parchment manuscript of the *Metamorphoses* of the eleventh century in the Laurentian Library in Florence is the oldest manuscript of this work. It once belonged to the Italian humanist Niccolò de' Niccoli and the Medici Library (San Marco 225). The first dated book was an edition of Ovid's works printed in Bologna, edited by Francesco da Pozzuoli and illuminated by Baldassare Azzoguidi. The date of this book, now in the Laurentian Library, is 1471. In the same library is a copy of the works of Ovid in perfect condition edited by Giovanni Andrea (Bussi), bishop of Aleria, dedicated to Paul II, and printed in Rome by Sweynheym and Pannartz in 1471.

VALERIUS MAXIMUS

Valerius Maximus wrote a book *Memorable Deeds and Sayings* in the reign of the Roman emperor Tiberius. Lifeless work that it is, it had a popularity in "educational" circles in even more lifeless abbreviations in the late Roman world and Middle Ages. His name rarely appears in catalogues of English collections before 1375, but commonly thereafter. The first chapter in the sixth book is concerned with chastity *(pudicitia)*. This state he terms "the particular foundation for men and women alike," *(virorum pariter ac feminarum praecipuum firmamentum)*. With words which guaranteed him a place in Christian esteem for centuries he sees in chastity the identifying qualities, the strength and the lasting bloom of youth:

> Tuo praesidio puerilis aetatis insignia munita sunt.
> Tui numinis respectu sincerus iuventae flos permanet.

> On your strength the identifying marks of youth are built. Under the generalship of your divinity the true flower of youth abides.

Lucretia is the only woman among the Roman examples of his topic. He tells her story of courage, will, and dignity *(fortitudo, constantia, gravitas)* with more pride than passion in seven unexciting lines. He succinctly points out the paradox of the will of a man in the body of a woman *(virilis animus . . . muliebre corpus)*, to which other Roman ladies were to be called to rise in the centuries to come because of dire historical events. Valerius Maximus made no contribution to the story. For his Christian readers none was needed. The story recommended itself on its own merits with the exception of one detail, the suicide.

A French translation of the text of Valerius Maximus on parchment by Simon de Hesdin and Nicolle de Gonesse (1469) in the Bibliothèque Nationale in Paris *(fr. 284)* accompanies the story of Lucretia with an illuminated miniature *(fol. 176)*. Two scenes are depicted. In one, Sextus has pulled the covers from Lucretia, semi-recumbent and nude except for a necklace, and he threatens her with a huge sword. In the second scene, in the palace, amid three weeping ladies and four of her avengers (Brutus, her father Sp. Lucretius, and probably her husband and P. Valerius), in a state of shock and prayer, Lucretia takes her life with a dagger.[6]

About the year 40 A.D. the Roman philosopher Seneca wrote a thoughtful essay for Marcia, the daughter of one of Sejanus' victims, to console her over the loss of her son. In this essay he disparages any attempt to place the inborn faculties and virtues of women on a lower plane than those of men. For women have equal energy and an equal capacity for the honorable, and they can bear equal pain and toil. In what city, he asks, could such a statement be more appropriately made than in Rome? He cites the role of Lucretia and Brutus in expelling a king from their city. Freedom, he continues, we owe to Brutus, and Brutus to Lucretia. (Bruto libertatem debemus, Lucretiae Brutum.) Seneca also cites Cloelia and the two Cornelias. Times were coming in both the pagan and the Christian world when woman was to be given the opportunity to demonstrate the inborn qualities attributed to her; and a millennium later the sparks of an ebbing fire had to be rekindled by a new set of apologists who knew their history. Thus, through his comfort to Marcia (*Dialogi* 6.16.2), Seneca deserves a place in the tradition of those who have striven to preserve the nobility of the human spirit in whatever crisis.

FLORUS

The Roman writer Florus of the second Christian century wrote an *Epitome of Roman History*. His main source was Livy. His allusions to Lucretia[7] are on the level of historical record and have no artistic merit. He identifies cruelty and lust (*libido*) as the cause of the Tarquins'[8] downfall. When he states that the husband of Lucretia, for no other reason than that of high birth, was stripped of power and banished from Rome, a victim of the people's exercise of their newly won freedom, he anticipates by many centuries the excesses of the democratic spirit throughout Europe in its struggle against narrowly held authority. The germination of dry seeds brings one to the very heart of the Renaissance. The wide use of Florus' work at one time as a school text contributed to the survival and popularity of the story of Lucretia. With the advent of printing this work continued to be popular. Printed editions in different parts of Europe followed one upon another after 1470. As will be seen later, Florus made creative writing unnecessary for the Christian annalist Jordanes in the sixth century.

PLUTARCH

In his essay on the virtues of women (*Moralia* 250a) Plutarch mentions the virtue of Lucretia and the insolence which it provoked even in violation of the code of hospitality as the cause of Lucretia's death and of Tarquin's expulsion.

CASSIUS DIO

Cassius Dio was a Greek historian who lived in the orbit of the Roman Empire, and who composed his *History of Rome* in Greek in the early part of the third Christian century. The Byzantine chronicler of the twelfth century, Zonaras, followed Cassius Dio closely in his *Compendium of History,* at least for the Roman period, and he occasionally compensates for the fragmentary text of Cassius Dio.

In telling once more the story of Lucretia, Cassius Dio (2.13-19) adopts the version of Livy and Ovid: that a discussion regarding the virtue of their wives had arisen among the men at camp, and that consequently they had decided to make a quick and unannounced visit to their homes, with the results found in Livy and Ovid. Sextus may have conceived a love for Lucretia because of her beauty and chastity, but it was her honor which he wanted to corrupt more than her body. He selected a time during the absence of her husband at which to ask for the hospitality due a kinsman, in order to violate Lucretia. There is no mention of his going to her bedroom for the violation. When neither persuasion nor force moved his victim, he succeeded in breaking her will by the stratagem of threatening to place her body beside that of a dead slave. In three statements Cassius Dio emphasizes the forced consent of Lucretia to the violation.

EUTROPIUS

If Cassius Dio enlivened history with rhetorical embellishments, Eutropius in the second half of the fourth century was content with a passionless *Breviary of Roman History*, which, if considered useful for schools, hardly recognizes the vital needs of young minds in their formative years. In a brief and unengaging paragraph (1.8) Eutropius reviews the expulsion of the Tarquins from Rome after the violation of Lucretia.

CHRISTIAN FATHERS

The Christian fathers found Lucretia's experience a useful instrument of Christian morality, even without any further adornment. Lucretia posed for them two questions: the guilt involved in the loss of chastity under force, and the attitude toward suicide, even under the circumstances. In the pagan world Lucretia and Cato chose suicide, one for personal and the other for political reasons. The fate of virgins in a world subject to barbarian invasions was a source of worry not only to those concerned, but also to the Christian fathers. Some women preferred suicide as a means of preserving their chastity. The tide of events had now brought back, as in the Rome of Lucretia, a strict observance of personal chastity, with an added excoriation of sex, but now as part of the Christian discipline. For those of the Christian fathers who wished to endorse the discipline the story of Lucretia served as an excellent example. And yet, the barbarian invasions in the Roman world posed for the Church the problem of its attitude toward the women who against their will fell victims to the invaders. Support for its decision in this matter was found in Greek philosophy.

The Church father Tertullian in his *Exhortation to Chastity* and in his essay *Monogamy* cites Dido and Lucretia as defenders of the ideal of monogamy. Those who submit to the infirmity of the flesh will have to face them as judges. Dido, he says, preferred to burn rather than to marry Iarbas. Lucretia atoned for her involuntary guilt by taking her own life.[8]

In his *Apology* (1.4) Tertullian mentions the instruments which attack the will of a Christian through the infirmity of his body: the sword, the cross, the fury of beasts, fire, and torture. But he reminds his Christian readers that some staunch men and women actually seek out these tortures as a means of achieving fame and glory. Lucretia was his example.[9]

St. Jerome (*ca.* 340–420) made a comment on the expulsion of Tarquin from Rome caused by his son's violation of Lucretia, in his revision of the second book of Eusebius' *Chronicle.* He observes that Tarquin instituted the use of chains, the whip, the cudgel, the quarry, prison, exile, etc., as means of coercion.[10]

St. Augustine (354–430) found it difficult to condemn those who staunchly defended the Christian ideals of chastity and monogamy, but he is uncompromising in his rejection of suicide even under such circumstances. In the *Problem of Free Choice* (3.8.23) he condemns suicide as a misguided act of ingratitude to the Creator. In the *City of God* (1.17) he expresses pity for those who found in self-destruction an avoidance of guilt for the loss of chastity. Furthermore, he said that no condemnation should be made of those who refuse to commit suicide under the circumstances. Forcible violation of a woman is no justification of her suicide (1.18). Lucretia, if innocent, had no right to commit suicide (1.19). Before the judges of the lower world she has no defense. St. Augustine then quotes lines from the sixth book of Vergil's *Aeneid* which refer to the sad lot of those in the lower world who, though innocent, inflicted death on themselves. "How glad they would be," says Vergil, "now in the upper air to bear to the full a humble life and bitter travails." But Fate and the barriers of Hades block them (*Aen.* 6.434-439). The glory of chastity may continue in the living bodies of those defiled by force. They should think only of the eyes of God. The act of Lucretia, he states, has been debated on both sides. But he reiterates his position (1.19), that Christians have no authority to commit suicide. St. Augustine notes (1.22) Plato's condemnation of suicide. Early in the *Phaedo* Socrates, sitting in prison on the morning of his execution, tells his friends that the gods are our guardians, and that we are in their hands and have no right, even should death be better than life, to open the door and run away. In order to remove any justification from the suicide of Lucretia as the cause of later historical events St. Augustine states (3.15) that the expulsion of Tarquin was not caused by Sextus' violation of Lucretia, since the father had nothing to do with this act of his son. St. Augustine, outspoken antagonist of Pelagius, fourth-century theologian from the British Isles, might have found a small area of agreement with the Pelagian formula that there has been no sin, if it is an act of necessity: Si necessitatis est, peccatum non est.

The thoughts of St. Augustine on the subject were given wide circulation by the publication of an elaborate commentary on the *City of God* (1522) by the Spanish author Ioannes Lodovicus Vives, a friend of Erasmus, who, indeed, suggested the work to Vives.

A century later (1640) George Rivers wrote a series of biographies in prose, among them that of Lucretia. In it he endorsed the point of view of St. Augustine.

A beautiful illuminated manuscript of St. Augustine's *City of God* in vellum is in part at The Hague and in part at Nantes in France. Its date is about 1478. The manuscript is a French translation and commentary for this work of St. Augustine made by Raoul de Praelles. The miniatures and the descriptions of them reveal that the manuscript is a striking amplification of a manuscript in the Bibliothèque Nationale in Paris, of the year 1473 (Gaucourt Ms. 18, 19 *franç.*). An extensive knowledge of the ancient authors is revealed in The Hague-Nantes manuscript. The commentator, however, mentions neither Herodotus nor Livy, though many of his sources are mentioned by name. The manuscript originally had 22 large miniatures and 638 small ones. They make an exciting addition to the text. Two miniatures of Lucretia accompany the text at chapter 19 of book 1(*folio* 23). One portrays the violation of Lucretia and her suicide, and the other the gathering of Romans before her corpse.[11]

The Gaucourt manuscript in Paris was the inspiration for two other illuminated manuscripts of the same work of St. Augustine by the same commentator, one in the Bibliothèque Sainte-Geneviève (Ms. 246) with miniatures of Maître François, who also did the miniatures of The Hague-Nantes manuscript, and the other in Mâcon (Ms. 1-2).

OROSIUS

Orosius was a Christian chronicler from Spain, and a contemporary of St. Augustine. He dedicated to St. Augustine a work called *History against the Pagans,* which attempts, by pointing out the calamities of man in pagan times, to defend the Christian faith against the charge of causing similar troubles in the present. Orosius included in his *History* (2.4.12) a brief review of the causes of resentment which built up against Tarquin and his son, and which resulted in the creation of a republican form of government. This document carried the name of Lucretia into the Middle Ages, and, through its first publication in 1471, into the Renaissance. It has been observed that Orosius did not use the text of Livy itself, but a lost epitome of it.[12]

JORDANES

Jordanes wrote his *Roman History* in the mid-sixth century. He notes lust as the last indignity which the Roman people could bear from the family of Tarquin. Lucretia sought atonement for the disgrace imposed upon her by taking her own life, and the expulsion of the regal authority followed. This passage of Jordanes was copied verbatim from the text of Florus.[13] Jordanes' originality consists in the omission of the word *tum* from a passage of several lines. In point of fact, a large portion of this work of Jordanes is lifted verbatim from Florus' text. There is also a noticeable improvement in the quality of his Latin in this part of his text. In their violent reaction against the kings and in their joy for their new-found freedom the people dismissed from the city one of their own consuls, the husband of Lucretia, simply because of his name and lineage.[14]

OTTO OF CLUNY

Otto (Odo), abbot of the monastery of Cluny, and once associated with the celebrated monastery of St. Martin at Tours, lived in the period around 879–942. Like St. Jerome he was torn between love and fear of anything as delightful, but, unfortunately, non-Christian, as Vergil and Boethius. He wrote an extensive Latin poem in seven books called *Occupatio* exposing the evil of the world. Even for a Christian there was only one good education: a pagan education learned through Latin. Here at the end of the Carolingian Renaissance Vergil, Horace, Juvenal, St. Ambrose, St. Augustine, Prudentius, Sedulius, and Gregory call Odo to expression in Latin verse. Turning his strictures against women guilty of adultery he reminded them that Lucretia preferred to avoid this disgrace through suicide (4.164), an act not sanctioned by one of Otto's principal sources, St. Augustine.

PETRUS COMESTOR

Peter the Voracious, a French biblical commentator and chronicler of the late twelfth century, makes an entry in his *Scholastic History* (*Book of Daniel,* chap. 19) concerning Tarquin the Proud and the violation of Lucretia as an event contemporary with Cyrus the Great. He observes that Tarquin had devised several forms of torture, which are specified. Entries of this sort he obtained in St. Jerome's *Chronica* and in Josephus.

WALTER MAP

Walter Map was a medieval ecclesiastic, man of the world, and commentator on centemporary court life in England at

the end of the twelfth century, in his work *On Courtiers'
Trifles (De Nugis Curialium)*. One of his recurring themes
is the venality of women. Lucretia still stands out in his
experience as a splendid example of self-imposed chastity.
With her in one of his tales he contrasts the specious chastity
of a queen of the Asiatics. In a tirade against woman he
singles out Lucretia and Penelope as exceptions to otherwise
general feminine immodesty, concluding that such noble
women do not exist any longer. His advice is to fear the
whole sex.[15]

BALLADS

The repertories of the ballad singers of the early Middle
Ages included legends of Greece and Rome. Vergil, Ovid,
and Livy are among the literary sources of their songs. In the
Trecento the Christian mother surrounded by her children
and loom at the family hearth found a deep spiritual affinity
with the chaste Lucretia.[16]

ROMANCE OF THE ROSE

The *Romance of the Rose* was an allegorical romance of
some 22,000 verses written in French in the thirteenth century, partly by Guillaume de Lorris. It uses the story of
Lucretia (8561-8660) in a way characteristic of this work.
The Titus Livy version (8612) is followed. Penelope and
Lucretia are mentioned in the *Romance of the Rose* (8605,
8608) in a diatribe against marriage. Rich or poor, beautiful
or ugly, it maintains, any woman will yield to the skilled
approach. It is an Ovidian point of view, less artistically
expressed. Penelope, the best woman in Greece, is no exception. Livy's version of Lucretia's violation, including the legal
distinction between the violated body and the pure heart,
and her refusal to absolve herself from guilt are then recounted. Lucretia still wanted to set a precedent for other
women and an example for men. The passage closes with
a sigh that there are no Penelopes and Lucretias any more.

The Fitzwilliam Museum in Cambridge, England, has a fourteenth-century vellum manuscript of the *Romance of the Rose,* which contains a miniature of Lucretia, with yellow hair, scarlet gown, and green head-dress, as she plunges a dagger into her breast. She is supported by her husband and her father.[17]

The influence of the *Romance of the Rose* found expression in the late fifteenth century in William Dunbar, sometimes called the Chaucer of Scotland. But his poem in praise of woman reflects the independent and sane judgment of writers in the British Isles on the matter.

Euripides put on the lips of Medea a pathetic acklowledgment of the helplessness of woman in a world of men. Some day, Medea cried, woman will come into her own—in song! Nor did the Middle Ages provide a sympathetic or encouraging climate for the development of feminine capabilities. A retreat to the nunnery was a common solution for a woman who was young, beautiful, or rich to avoid the brutality of men. A spirited discussion and appraisal of woman's capabilities was the concern of the later medieval writers. Livy has rendered an important service in human progress by handing down this dramatic example of self-sustaining dignity and resolve in a lady of early Roman society. This beacon of feminine independence was never extinguished by the vituperation of woman during the Middle Ages. While it shone forth, there was hope for Western woman.

The prosperity which Europe experienced in the thirteenth century as a result of the Crusades and of the rebirth of trade was to affect materially the place of woman in Western society. Through Sicily, Lucca, and Florence, after the twelfth century, a steadily increasing flow of eastern luxuries—silks, jewels, and perfumes—came to Europe, lending to woman a new attractiveness, and drawing to her a new admiration and a new articulateness regarding not only her nobility, but also her irresistible charm.

The thirteenth century witnessed the rapid growth of Florence from a small town to one of the powerful cities of Europe.

But the remoteness of Livy is evident in the variant spellings of his name in the manuscripts of the *Romance of the Rose*, such as "Chinilivius," "Tivilinius," and even "Thitus li vieus."

TRANSMITTING DOCUMENTS OF EARLY RENAISSANCE

Manuscripts of Livy existed in modest numbers in the medieval libraries, but he generally tended to be only a name in a list. Manitius lists over 50 manuscripts of Livy in Germany, France, Italy, Spain, and England.[18] The Bodleian Library at Oxford has a manuscript of the first nine books of Livy's *History,* dating about the year 1000. But John of Salisbury, despite his wide reading in the Classics, did not know Livy's text at first hand. To Boston of Bury in medieval England, whose *Cathologus* survives, Livy seems known only remotely. Livy's name appears in the lists of two English catalogues of the thirteenth century, and thereafter not until the fifteenth century, at Oxford.[19] An edition of Livy in perfect condition and with colored initials is part of the collection of the Laurentian Library in Florence. It was edited by Giovanni Andrea (Bussi), bishop at Aleria, and printed in Rome by Sweynheym and Pannartz in 1469, as the *editio princeps* of Livy. The bishop was a friend of Laurentius Valla.

A translation of Livy into French by Petrus Berchorius, in the middle of the fourteenth century, gave Livy a wider circulation. A parchment manuscript of this translation, of about the year 1380, is in The Hague, and another in the Bibliothèque Nationale in Paris. The illuminated illustrations of the latter manuscript, reminiscent of the style of the fifteenth-century French painter, illuminator, and miniaturist Foucquet, are unusual in their antiquarian interest in providing at this early time authentic costumes and monuments of the Roman period.[20]

DANTE

Dante makes two passing references to Lucretia: once when he sees her in the exalted company of noble spirits (*Inferno* 4.128), and again to mention her grief in regal times in Rome (*Paradiso* 6.41).

PETRARCH

Petrarch (1304–1374) came to the story of Lucretia through his fresh knowledge of Roman history and a life-long study of parts of the text of Livy. The text of Livy known by Laurentius Valla to have been owned and annotated by Petrarch in his own hand has been shown to be the Harleian Ms. 2493 in the British Museum. Petrarch also wrote some of the first decade of this manuscript of Livy. The ultimate source of his corrections and notes seems to have been the important *codex Mediceus* in the Laurentian Library in Florence *(plut.* 63.19). Petrarch also possessed another Livy, now in Paris (Latin 5690).[21] In both the *Sonnets* and the *Triumphs* he refers to the nobility, courage, and virtue of Lucretia, carrying on the time-honored comparison of her with Penelope, Polyxena, and others. Loss of honor, he reflects, is worse than death; grief alone did not suffice for her (*Poems* 262). The influence of his *Triumphs* on the pictorial arts, as, *e.g.*, Luca Signorelli's *Triumph of Chastity,* gave Lucretia, who is included in this work, part of its own fame.[22] Among the manuscripts in the Bibliothèque Nationale in Paris there is a translation of Petrarch's *Triumphs,* with illuminated miniatures. A chariot in the *Triumph of Reason* is preceded by virtuous women, among them Virginia, Penelope, and, most prominent, Lucretia.[23]

Petrarch retold the story of Lucretia in his long Latin epic poem *Africa* (3.684-802). Within four verses he has moved to the violation. Obviously he is little more than an annalist here. Lucretia has by now acquired a Christian sense of sin. In Livy's account she is reported merely as being sad *(maesta)* after the violation. But in Petrarch's version she is not only

grief-stricken *(dolens)*, but she thoroughly hates both her life
and her body (3.691). She is angry at her limbs (692), and
thinks of herself as bearing forever the ugly stain of adultery
(693f.). She plans to lay aside in the presence of her father
and her husband the hated burden of her body (701). The
march of events of Petrarch's story matches that of Livy, but
there is only an occasional verbal reminiscence of Livy.
Petrarch tells the story in his own vocabulary.[24]

BOCCACCIO

Boccaccio narrates the story of Lucretia in about 50 lines
in his work *On Illustrious Women (De Claris Mulieribus)*,
written probably in the decade of 1363–1373, shortly before
the creative period of Gower and Chaucer. Over a hundred
ladies were selected for this hall of fame. Boccaccio holds
Lucretia up as a holy example of chastity. At the close of his
account he bestows upon her another due meed of praise,
mentions the revenge exacted for the criminal act of Sextus,
and notes the boon of freedom and liberty which came to
Rome from this wanton act of violence. In retelling the story
of Pyramus and Thisbe in this same work Boccaccio reveals
only slight hints of the original text of Ovid, but he proceeds
to relate the tale in his own way and vocabulary.[25] In contrast, however, his story of Lucretia is quite close to the text
of Livy in both content and vocabulary. Words and phrases
are repeated, sometimes in the same constructions.[26] After
following Livy closely Boccaccio at the end of his story lapsed
into half of a dactylic hexameter: *animam cum sanguine
fudit.*[27] Boccaccio goes beyond Livy's *corde* in declaring Lucretia innocent *(pectus innocuum)*, and he defends the heroine
at every turn of the story; but he departs from Livy's version
in having Lucretia, however unwillingly, offer Sextus her
body *(corpus permisit adultero)* because of his threat of bring-
ing down upon her a disgrace which she, if dead, would be
unable to disprove. Cassius Dio (2.16) also introduced the
element of permission on the part of Lucretia. Liking to probe

into causes as a guide to the future, Boccaccio found the cause of Lucretia's misfortune in her beauty.[28] He had been anticipated in this observation of the close relationship between the beauty and misfortune of Lucretia by Juvenal many centuries earlier:

> Sed vetat optari faciem Lucretia qualem
> ipsa habuit. (*Satires* 10.293f.)

> Lucretia herself forbids such beauty as she had to be an object of prayer.

Boccaccio's mood in this story is thoroughly wholesome and pious. Here at any rate he did not deserve the strictures directed against him a century-and-a-half later by Ioannes Lodovicus Vives, mentioned above in the discussion of St. Augustine. In his work *Instruction of a Christian Woman,* which went through over forty editions and translations by the end of the sixteenth century, Vives criticizes the subtleties and deceptions of popular tales and romances, singling out both Boccaccio and Poggio for specific mention. He recommends the Bible as reading preferable to Boccaccio. True, the licentiousness of the popular stories of France and Italy leaves little unsaid. But humor, good taste, and moral earnestness, especially in England, lifted the type into acceptable literary expression. Ovid was regarded by Vives as more dangerous than Plato supposedly regarded Homer and Hesiod to be. Vives' high regard for Justin, Florus, and Valerius Maximus justifies one's suspicion that he had no important contribution to make to literature. He was, however, an ardent champion of the emancipation of woman through a liberal Christian education.

There is an anonymous English translation of this work of Boccaccio belonging to the middle of the fifteenth century. The translation includes an allusion to Lydgate's *Fall of Princes,* written in the same period.[29]

Another link in the chain of transmission of this story is the translation of part of this work of Boccaccio by Lord Morley

(1546), a Christian humanist, and like Caxton a precursor of
better known subsequent translators of the Continental tradition. Lord Morley is a fine example of the receptive climate
provided by a devout Christian in England in the generation
before Shakespeare for the idealism of Livy, Horace, Cicero,
Seneca, and Plutarch. The high moral earnestness of classical
example now came to the Court of England in English. For
the ladies of the Court of Henry VIII, to whom Lord Morley
directed his translation, the story was intended as a dignified
educational experience. The climate of the Court on the subject of the story may be realized if one remembers that a
decade earlier Anne Boleyn, wife of Henry VIII, was condemned to death on a charge of adultery. The loose nature of
Lord Morley's handling of the Latin text is of little more than
academic interest. The laudatory nature of his exercise leaves
undeveloped in his translation, as in the original text, the
dramatic and artistic liveliness of Livy's version.

Through the exciting history of this work of Boccaccio in
the Renaissance Lucretia was to serve as an *exemplum,* imposing upon the man-woman relationship an absolute standard of honor and decency for both man and woman alike—a
tenuous goal which has ever corrected the traditional concept
of woman as a subject for exploitation.

Another of Boccaccio's Latin works, coming from the last
years of his life, was his *On the Misfortunes of Famous Men
and Women (De Casibus Virorum et Feminarum Illustrium).*
Within a context of universal history, from Adam to the time
of writing, Boccaccio formed from the experience of the past
for the violent political opportunism of his Italy a minatory
and monitory treatise of political philosophy. Like a Herodotus for his own day Boccaccio saw the fortunes of the great
subjected to a Wheel of Fortune and brought back to wisdom
and moderation by the misfortunes caused by their own ambition, greed, and licentiousness. The story of Lucretia was
convincing documentation. He retells it briefly, with only an
occasional verbal echo of Livy, and some contradictions.

The first printed edition of this work of Boccaccio appeared in 1475, exactly one century after his death. But long before this time an expanded translation of it in French prose was made by Laurent de Premierfait (d. 1418), under the title *Des nobles malheureux*. The British Museum has a vellum manuscript (18.750) of this translation of Boccaccio's work of the year 1409. The miniatures, however, include neither Lucretia nor Cyrus. The first printed edition of the French version was that of the famous Colard Mansion in Bruges in 1476, and several other editions appeared through the sixteenth century. The second edition (1483) was the first illustrated book published in Paris. Translations of the Latin document into French, German, Italian, and Spanish were many throughout the sixteenth century. Both Boccaccio and Laurent rationalized the divine and the miraculous; hence, when Laurent expanded his Latin original, if he did not draw upon his own experience, he preferred to go to Boccaccio's *De Genealogiis* rather than to Ovid.

GESTA ROMANORUM

The *Achievements of the Romans (Gesta Romanorum)* is a collection of moralized stories, fables, and parables which was very popular throughout Europe in both Latin and the vernacular languages, at first in manuscript form and later in printed editions. The oldest Latin edition of the *Gesta* appeared probably a generation before the opening of the sixteenth century. In its varied collection it gathered up the story of Lucretia (#135). The ethical problem of this early Roman heroine is here placed in a Christian context and given a Christian solution. The story opens with a reference to St. Augustine's use of it in the *City of God*, and there are echoes of Livy's version, but the picturesque, the dramatic, and the psychological qualities of the story as developed by Livy and Ovid are noticeably absent. Lucretia's husband has by now become "Calatinus" or later, "Colatinus." Sextus' passion for Lucretia came from a visit to the castle *(castrum)* of Calatinus.

Sextus selected a time for his visit when both Calatinus and
Tarquin were away from Rome. The historical and geograph-
ical setting of the original story have faded away. As in both
Livy and Ovid, there is the contrast of *hospes* and *hostis.* With
no reference to hospitality Sextus is reported to have spent
the night at the castle and to have secretly entered the cham-
ber of Lucretia. Livy's phrase *sinistraque manu mulieris
pectore oppresso* has become *manu sinestra opprimens pectus
eius;* and Livy's *iugulatum servum nudum* has become *servum
iugulatum nudum.* Whereas in Livy and Ovid Lucretia summoned her father and husband, in this medieval version she
summoned also her brothers, the emperor, those of her kinsmen designated by the vague Latin word *nepotes,* and the
proconsuls. In Livy's version tragedy is forecast when Lucretia asked her kinsmen what salvation there was for a
woman who has lost her chastity. Since the medieval version
of the story suggests a Christian solution, the medieval Lucretia is not allowed to make any such statement. But the
next sentence of Livy:

> Vestigia viri alieni, Collatine, in lecto sunt tuo

> The mark of a stranger, Collatinus, is on your couch

has been modified by a transcriber who either misread an
abbreviation or tried to improve the reading *vestigia,* for
Lucretia is reported to have said,

> Scias tu, o Colatine, vestimenta viri alieni in lecto
> tuo fuisse.

> You may know, Colatinus, that the clothing of a
> stranger has been on your couch.

Livy's next sentence,

> Ceterum corpus est tantum violatum, animus insons.

> But it is only my body which has been violated, and
> my mind is innocent.

is closely followed:

> Licet corpus sit violatum, animus tamen est inno-
> cens.

> Though my body has been violated, yet my mind is
> innocent.

In Livy's episode of the suicide Lucretia asks for revenge but
is in the bargain declared innocent. In the medieval version
she asks for acquittal. In both versions she holds herself to
the supreme penalty. In Livy she says,

> Me . . . supplicio non libero.

> I do not free myself from punishment.

and in the *Gesta,*

> A pena tamen non liberabor.

> Yet I shall not be freed from the penalty.

The medieval version now concludes quickly. Her kinsmen
and friends swear to expel the Tarquins, and Sextus is later
killed. No mention is made of Brutus.

The Christian application of the story is then developed.
Lucretia, being a noble lady, was bathed in the baptismal
waters of God and joined to Him. Sextus is the tempting devil
who enters her heart and soul. In the father, husband, and
friends of Lucretia the medieval narrator saw the confessor,
Christ, and holy men. Sins may be atoned through contrition,
confession, and service. Suicide should be through the sword
of repentance. The carrying of the body to Rome symbolizes
the entrance into the Holy Church. Sin and salvation yield to
the good life.

The dry crumbs of a once exciting ancient experience still
nourish the unrealistic medieval mind. A dehydrated antiquity with Christian seasoning still delights and educates
medieval man. The salvation and comfort denied to Lucretia
in the pagan authors are extended to her at least after death
in this medieval version.[30]

CHRISTINE DE PISAN

Christine de Pisan was an important Christian humanist of the early fifteenth century in France. The body of ancient experience which she transmitted from Italy to France and England she set in a Christian context of a moral and allegorical nature. She was also a lively example and champion of the emancipated woman.

The literature of the fifteenth century contains a full discussion of woman, based upon a new awareness of her place in ancient society, and upon conditions and relationships which the Middle Ages had denied to her. Euripides had observed centuries before (*Iphigenia Taurica* 1006) that the lot of woman was not a healthy one (*ta de gynaikos asthene*). Dozens of appraisals were made in the fifteenth century, and all known experience was used in them. Given the complexities of the subject, the conclusions regarding woman permitted the extremes of a Dantesque sublimation as well as of scurrilous detraction. Amid eulogy and venom the moral and physical aspects of the theme are not neglected. Any progress accomplished had always to overcome a traditional prejudice against woman and her just due in society. Aeneas Silvius Piccolomini of Siena (Pius II, 1508–1578), a statesman and scholar, wrote a dialogue (1538) in praise of woman which went through seven editions in its century. The opposite position, however, was taken by his contemporary, Michelangelo Biondo (1497–1565), whose discourse was entitled *Anguish, Grief, and Trouble, the Three Furies of the World*.[31] Lucretia, however, he deems a *raro lume di castità romana*. As in much else, Italy was the teacher of Europe on this important subject.

In her work *Cyte of Ladyes* (2.44), as an early English translation is entitled, revenge for Lucretia moves swiftly to inevitable retribution under divine justice and law. At the beginning of the story Christine defends ladies against a charge of licentiousness in enjoying the violation of their honor. Only for a time was Sextus Tarquin's passion for Lucretia restrained by a sense of shame. Unsuspectingly, in the absence of her husband Lucretia extended to her kinsman the dutiful hospitality which befitted his position and her sense of propriety. When she was awakened by her assailant in the dead of night, fear kept her motionless and speechless, which gave Sextus a chance to try to win her by promises, gifts, and offers. But even the threat of violence failed to win her consent. His proposed plan, however, to sully her good name in death with a charge of adultery forced her to submit. In the morning she explained all to her father, husband, and kin. As a result, Tarquin was banished, and the commendable law imposing death upon the violator of a woman's honor was thought by some to have originated in this incident.

The violation of Lucretia became useful to Christine de Pisan in her work *Lavision* (1405) as an example of God's manifest work against vice and evil. Troy fell because Paris had taken Helen there. The Tarquins were banished from Rome because of the violation of Lucretia's honor by Sextus. Hannibal, too, found ruin in his loss of honor. Thus, remote history and mythology serve as examples to hold temporal rulers to a strict accounting under the sovereignty of a liberal Christian humanism, especially for the benefit and protection of woman.

MACHIAVELLI

Machiavelli (1469–1527) was a keen student of not only Roman history, but also Livy, the eloquent spokesman of the Republic. His *Discourses* on the first decade of Livy was in print by 1531, and its popularity is attested by its translation into French and English. The *editio princeps* of Livy appeared in Rome in the year of Machiavelli's birth. The British Museum has an edition of Livy published in Venice in 1501, and one published in Germany in 1518. Livy was translated into Italian by 1476, into French by 1487, into German by 1505, into Spanish by 1520, into Dutch by 1541, and into English by 1600. In the experience of the ancient Romans

Machiavelli found guidance and advice for the turbulent
Florence of his day. In the wise prudence of Brutus' feigned
witlessness he saw the justification of expedience, since
Brutus survived the tyranny and lived to rid his country of it.
The violation of Lucretia was the spark which touched off
the explosive protest against the cruelty and arrogance of
Tarquin. Brutus was the first to pull the dagger from the
wound of Lucretia, and to bind her kinsmen by oath not to
tolerate kings in Rome. But a guide to safe action against a
ruler lies in an appraisal of his power and in subservience to
him, if necessary.[32] Shrewd rulers should realize that women
have been the cause of many troubles, and that such troubles
should be scrupulously avoided.[33] For men are willing to
fight and die in defense of their women.

BANDELLO

An important transmitting instrument of Renaissance en-
thusiasms superimposed on old stories is the *Tales* (*Novelle*,
1554) of Matteo Bandello (*ca.* 1480–1562). His stories were
extremely popular, and found their way from their Italian
prose into French and English (1579) translations and frequent adaptations in Elizabethan and Shakespearean drama.
Bandello was keenly aware of the stern and heroic legacy of
ancient Rome, the light of which illuminated the unworthi-
ness of the present to deserve comparison. Taking a position
in the lively appraisal of woman's merits in the countries
being affected by the Renaissance, he was frank enough to
state that at least men were no better than the detractors
of women judged women to be. Quite the contrary, Paolina
was one of those rare persons who exemplified supremely the
ancient ideal of virtue in woman by her sincere love for her
husband and attention to the domestic arts. She was in no
way inferior to those classic examples of ancient virtue in the
home—Lucretia and Cornelia (3.19).

One of Bandello's tales (1.8) related the tragedy of Giulia
da Gazuolo. The story is a sensual narration of the seduction

and forced violation of the honor of a girl who, though innocent, found refuge from her shame by drowning herself.
Bandello judged her to be no less praiseworthy than Lucretia,
and possibly more so.

In another tale (2.21) of a dozen pages of intense prose he
narrates once more, as a romanticized Livy, the violation of
Lucretia by Sextus Tarquin.

LYDGATE

An important extension of Boccaccio's *De Casibus* into
the cultural stream of the West is John Lydgate's *Fall of
Princes* (1431). It is a condensed paraphrase of the work of
Laurent de Premierfait. There is no evidence of the use of
the Latin original by Lydgate. His work has the distinction
of being one of the first pieces of English literature to enjoy
an extension into other languages, for versions of it appeared
in Spanish, Italian, German, and French.

The Roman heroine Lucretia furnished illustrative material
in the ramifications of this expression of comparative literature. The examples held up to the world in this work of
Lydgate are pagan and Christian, Greek, Roman, and Hebrew. Christian humanism has synthesized them. In terms
of availability of text it is easier to find the Lucretia of this
tradition in her English form than in the French or Latin.
But the variations are slight. Lydgate's version, however,
gives an insight into the definition of woman's place in the
society represented by the author of the text.

Lucretia, along with Penelope, emerges in the first book of
Lydgate's *Fall of Princes* from a section devoted to the malice
of women (6511-6706). Lydgate follows identical passages
in Laurent and Boccaccio.[34] The latter's passage begins
bluntly:

Blandum et exitiabile malum mulier.

Woman is a flattering and pernicious evil.

Lydgate only hesitantly commended Boccaccio for his attack on women. He professes to become very weary of Boccaccio's rehearsal of examples, and refuses in fairness to condemn all for the depravity of a few. He abbreviated considerably the expanded treatment of the topic found in the text of Laurent, and made the constructive suggestion that virtuous women should be all the more honored for their virtue by contrast with the rest. His feminine readers would no doubt have already anticipated his remark that men are no better than women. The Middle Ages provided a poor environment for women, high or low, rich or poor, old or young, to develop their various capabilities. Boccaccio may complain of women in nunneries, but often it was their safest refuge from violence. Lydgate's final thought on the matter was that good women should

> lihtli passe, and ther sleuys shake, (6704)

since Boccaccio was not writing about them at all. Lucretia and Penelope are examples whose

> noble fame abrood doth syne and spreede. (6731)

In behalf of Boccaccio it should be noted that he too sweetened his vitriol with a touch of honey by making practically the same reservations to his denunciation as Lydgate made. Boccaccio was aware of certain women, both Christian and pagan, who merited only the highest praise and should be extolled more than men. But his parting thought qualifies his qualification as follows:

> Quoniam rarissimae sunt: ne, dum Lucretiam quaeris, in Calpurniam aut Semproniam cadas. Omnes fugiendas censeo, debito posteritati concesso.

> Since such women are very rare, do not, in seeking a Lucretia, fall upon a Calpurnia or a Sempronia. I propose that they should all be avoided, our obligation to posterity being granted.

In a long passage (967-1344) in the second book Lydgate

returns to the story of Lucretia. He notes (980) that Chaucer has written a "legende soverayne." He is torn between a sense of the presumptuousness of retelling the story after Chaucer and of the pity of hiding it (1003). But there was the practical matter that his lord had bidden him to translate

the doolful processe off hir pitous fate, (1008)

and probably Lord Humphrey had placed in Lydgate's hands a still extant declamation on the subject of Collucyus (Colucio Salutato), friend of Petrarch. Lydgate also had at hand the text of Laurent. The emphasis in this version of the story is on the political repercussions of the violation. The story of the violation itself is told in 16 lines. Sextus came upon her like a thief, but there are no details regarding the "where" or "why." In the version of Laurent, Collatinus was a Roman nobleman. After Sextus threatened Lucretia by saying that he would involve her with a churl, she submitted.

Then follows a passage of some 300 lines (1058-1330) in which the legal, sociological, and psychological aspects of the situation are explored in two monologues. The father and husband both excuse and comfort her. They recall her domestic fidelity on that fateful night when she was spinning with her maids. She was trapped like a fowl in a snare. Only her body, not her soul, was corrupted, and Sextus found her like a stone image. There will be revenge. Not only is there no guilt on her part, but indeed, to die, under the circumstances, would be a confession of guilt and a blameworthy act. But in her monologue Lucretia saw no reason to set a bad social example, to live in shame, and to disgrace her family and children. With a puritanical fear of there having been possibly some unwitting delight in her trespass she shows herself an adept student of mythology by calling on the gods and goddesses of chastity, and on Minos and Rhadamanthus, who will judge her soul, and with a call to vengeance on her lips she dies by her own hand. The revenge on the ruling family was not long in coming.

Lydgate returns to the story of Lucretia in book three (932-1148). He professes to follow Boccaccio at this point, and recommends this character study as approved reading. After her violation, Lucretia clad herself in black, and spoke to her father, husband, and friends. She begins her story with the arrival of Sextus as a guest, as she was spinning in the castle with her maids. She points out the obligation of a king's son and a knight to protect women. Instead of that, this violator of both civil law and family bonds came like a lion in the dark of night and forced her, on the threat of death. She speaks of her shame, of the need for revenge as a deterrent to future adulterers, and of her possible guilt. She was at once absolved, and committed suicide. At this point Lydgate reports Boccaccio's bitter tirade against those who bring the law of nature on innocent women. Classical examples are cited of high standards of morality which princes should follow. Lydgate has in reality followed Laurent closely in this passage, apart from omissions. He has omitted Laurent's account of the banquet at Ardea preceding the visit to the wives, and also Sextus' threat to kill a servant and implicate Lucretia in guilt with him. Lucretia's black raiment Lydgate derived from some other source than Laurent.[35] Ultimately it went back to Dionysius of Halicarnassus and Ovid.

The only other reference to Lucretia in this work of Lydgate is in the seventh book (439-445). Here Messalina, pleading before Caligula and Tiberius, admits her guilt, but only if it is appraised against the high standards of Lucretia's self-imposed discipline.

A manuscript of this work of Lydgate in the British Museum (Harley 1766) illustrates the violation of Lucretia with a miniature (101v.). Lucretia lies on a couch which is adorned with a canopy of blue draperies and a red and gilded crown on top. She is covered with a red blanket. Tarquin in armor restrains her with his left hand, and wields a large sword with his right hand. Another miniature (105r.) shows her in a forest plunging a sword into her breast.

GOWER

John Gower was a contemporary and friend of Chaucer. His *Lover's Confession (Confessio Amantis)* had roots in the *Romance of the Rose,* and was, in turn, among the first pieces of English literature to be translated into a Continental tongue. Gower tells the story of Lucretia in the seventh book (4754-5130). There are only minor deviations from the version of Ovid. Arrons (Aruns), a son of Tarquin, started a discussion regarding the wives at home. The young men were in disguise when they came to the palace at Rome. Gower finds his strength as a narrator when he describes Lucretia tearfully complaining of her husband's absence, and the return of beauty to her face when he appeared, though he can hardly match the effective brevity of Ovid's verse

deque viri collo dulce pependit onus.

She hung from the neck of her husband—a sweet burden.

Gower pauses over the young Tarquin, as he was being entertained by his unsuspecting kinswoman, long enough to compare him with a tiger biding his time for the kill. When he seized her, he took her in both his arms. Little is said on either side. He threatened to slay her and those around her. Since she immediately swooned, she was unable to ponder a course of action as she did in Ovid, or to hear any plea he might have prepared, or even the traditional threat of implicating her with a slain servant. A later day gives them both more eloquence. Following a tradition which Ovid knew from the *Hecuba* of Euripides (568-570), and which he extended to the dying Lucretia (*Fasti* 2.833f.) and to Polyxena (*Metamorphoses* 13.479f.), Gower permitted Lucretia to arrange her clothes in falling so that no man should see her knees. The association of Lucretia with Penelope (8.2621-2631) has by this time become a commonplace.

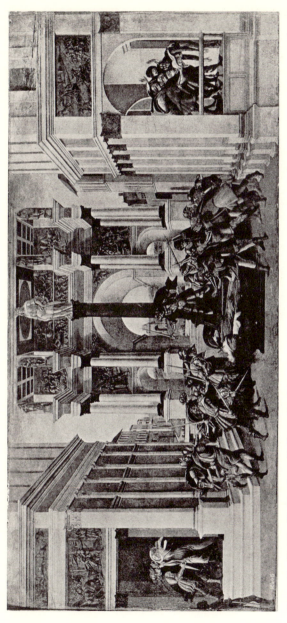

Lucretia. Botticelli. Gardner Gallery, Boston

Lucretia. Lorenzo Lotto. National Gallery, London

CHAUCER

In his *Legend of Good Women* Chaucer (1340–1400) cites his authorities for the story of Lucretia: Ovid, Livy, and St. Augustine. He also knew this story in the *Romance of the Rose,* which he translated, and he obviously had his eye on the references to Lucretia in this work (8605-8612) when he wrote lines 1080-1085 in the *Book of the Duchess.* But from the first line of Chaucer's story in the *Legend of Good Women:*

Now moot I seyn the exiling of kinges (1.1680),

which is a translation of the first line of Ovid's story:

nunc mihi dicenda est regis fuga (*Fasti* 2.685),

these two admirers of the feminine spirit were together.

The departures from Ovid are few. Chaucer's story takes place in Rome, instead of in Collatia. So also in the *Gesta Romanorum.* (The Middle Ages would be less clear about geography than was Ovid.) As a protection of the good name of women no allusion is made by Chaucer to Sextus' prior visit to the palace and to the carousing of the royal women. For the men go directly to the house of Calatinus. Chaucer cites Livy as authority that Lucretia was working her "soft wool." As a matter of fact, the phrase *lanaque mollis* is Ovid's (*Fasti* 2.742). Chaucer has here expanded one line of Ovid into seven. In Chaucer's version Sextus did not avail himself of the hospitality accorded to a kinsman when he made his criminal visit to seduce Lucretia. For he came to the house of Calatinus quite secretly. In the *Gesta Romanorum,* too, Sextus simply spent the night at the castle, with no reference to hospitality, and he secretly entered the bedchamber of Lucretia. Under the influence of shame and fear because completely trapped by Sextus, Lucretia swooned, thus relieving herself of any charge of consent. In Chaucer's version Lucretia summons her mother as well as her father and husband. Patriarchal authority is indeed extended.

With a few interpolations the Lucretia of Ovid could be made over into a steadfast Christian wife. Possibly through an extension of Ovid (*Fasti* 2.842) Chaucer has given to early Republican Rome her first saint, forgiving her for the unchristian act of commiting suicide. Chaucer's story, denying the misogynism of the *Romance of the Rose*, is a defense not only of Lucretia, but of women generally, and of their capacity to live and die for a trust. Had not Christ himself paid similar tribute to women? Instead of complimenting Lucretia, as did Ovid, by attributing to her the courage of a man (*Fasti* 2.847) Chaucer reprimands men for their tryanny and brutality. Sextus, too, is rebuked for his failure to abide by the code of chivalry and honor imposed on him by his birth.

OTHER ENGLISH WRITERS

This important social value judgment regarding the place and potential of woman in society continued to be assessed in England for a long time. John Rastell, one of Sir Thomas More's circle in the early sixteenth century, and a writer, producer, and printer of plays, printed a play on Lucretia, which survives in fragmentary form. A poem of Thomas Feylde called *Contraversye* (*ca.* 1508) attacks the frailty and inconstancy of woman.[36] Medea and Lucretia gave woman a bad name. He comments:

> Mulier est hominis confusio.

> Woman gets the human race all mixed up.

On the other hand, Vives published in London in 1523 a manual for the education of girls *(De ratione studii puerilis);* and a poem possibly to be attributed to Robert Vaughan maintains the perfection of woman. In Vaughan's opinion wicked women are the creation of men, and virtue is more natural to women than to men.[37] Thomas Elyot's *Defence of Good Women* appeared in London in 1540 and thereafter.[38]

In 1560 Edward More published a "a lytle and bryefe treatyse, called the defence of women, and especially of Englyshe women." He urged young men to marry, blaming the fall of man on Adam, not on Eve. He places English women on a higher plane than Roman women, but reminds his readers that even Rome had Lucretia and Ovid's loyal wife. He cites examples from the Scriptures and includes false men like Aeneas in the Vergil known to the Middle Ages. The vices of men he regards as greater than those of women.[39] Sir Thomas Wyatt (1503–1542), English statesman and love poet with attachment to Italian sources, found Lucretia not so much an example of public morality as a useful illustration of the ceaseless cares of love.

VIVES

Ioannes Lodovicus Vives (1492–1540) was born in Valencia, Spain, and educated in Paris. He became a friend of Erasmus, a widely read student of the Classics, and a devout Christian disciple. Through his friendship with Erasmus and Sir Thomas More he won distinction in England and at the Court in the early twenties of the sixteenth century, serving as preceptor of Princess Mary. His career and writings show him to be a cosmopolitan humanist in an age when new horizons were opening in not only geography, but also in social perspectives. Vives' work *On the Training of Christian Women (De Institutione Foeminae Christianae,* 1523) not only created a new image of woman in society, but served as a pedagogical manual in which a humanistic integration of pagan and Christian experience provided a mirror in which the image might be seen. This work went through eight editions by the end of the eighteenth century, and was copiously translated into French, German, and Spanish. In the exposition of his topic Vives drew with ease upon the whole range of Greek and Roman pagan literature and the Latin Christian fathers. Few are the authors whom he fails to use, from Homer to Plutarch and from Plautus to St. Jerome.

The length of the list of itself discourages its recital here. Strangely enough, the name of Herodotus seems to be missing.

HYRDE

An extension of the influence of Vives and a tribute to his popularity and usefulness in his time is seen in the English translation of his work by Richard Hyrde called *Instruction of a Christen Woman*. Hyrde spent four years on his translation, and it went into nine editions between 1529 and 1592. Hyrde found himself in agreement with the growing liberal awareness of woman's potential. The medieval venom against her has been rejected. Lucretia, of course, is well known to both Vives and Hyrde. Quintilian (5.11.10) is cited as a source for the story.[40] Suicide, however, is not recommended. With chastity, says Hyrde, woman has everything. But though she has everything, "calle her a noughty packe," and she has nothing. Regarding Ovid, one of the original sources of the story, Hyrde is of two minds, but in one mood he calls Ovid "a schole maister of baudry, and a common corrupter of vertue."

PAINTER

A popular collection of tales available to the Elizabethans was *The Palace of Pleasure* (1566-1575) of William Painter. In its final form it contained 100 stories in prose culled from Herodotus, Aelian, Plutarch, Livy, Tacitus, Aulus Gellius, Quintus Curtius, and from French and Italian sources. Stories of seduction and adultery are well represented. Herodotus is represented in this text by the stories of Candaules and Gyges and of Croesus and Solon. The story of Cyrus and Panthea, once delightfully told by Xenophon in his *Education of Cyrus*, had a more recent source in Matteo Bandello (*Novelle* 3.9). Among the six stories from Livy is that of Lucretia. In Livy's account of the incident Lucretia said to her husband: Vestigia viri alieni, Collatine, in lecto sunt tuo. In Painter's version Lucretia says, "Alas Collatine, the steppes of an other man, be now fixed in thy bed." Lucretia's kinsmen in Livy's story comforted her by saying that when intent was missing, guilt was lacking too. Painter writes, "Where consent was not, there the crime was absente." In the end it was for the kinsmen to avenge "the mischiefe of that facinorous rape." With its record of sensationalism and criminal bestiality this book of Painter satisfied a hunger in a nation whose energy exceeded its experience. The Elizabethan playwrights turned to these stories of Painter for topics.

DRAMA, BALLADS

Lucretia was a favorite figure in baroque drama of the Continent also.[41] One of the medieval dramas on Lucretia was printed in 1530. Ballads on the story of Lucretia registered in 1568 and 1569 also helped to familiarize the English-reading public with this Roman legend. Just as the ancient world provided the medieval world with a humanistic base for a Christian way of life, so in its proper time it provided the Renaissance with a broad base of experience from which it might extend itself into the realm of goods and desires.

PETTIE

John Pettie wrote his *Petite Pallace of Pleasure* (1576) for the delight and instruction of gentlewomen. It was a collection of stories, mainly from Ovid, but with echoes of Livy, Hyginus, Tacitus, Cicero, Horace, Publilius Syrus, Erasmus, and the Bible, and with a continental interest in love and women. There was at that time no better mirror in which woman might see herself than that provided by the societies of Greece and Rome. Once woman ceased to be a victim of political and social conditions, it was in the best interests of men, too, as well as of women, that they be re-educated and replaced in society as men would want them. Pettie's attitude toward woman was constructive. She should allow no compromise of her chastity and honor. Penelope and Lucretia are commended for their steadfastness and courage. It was

in the best interests of man to accept woman's frailties along
with his own, and to protect her by law from abuse. Lucretia
contributed to the awareness in the Renaissance of the
emancipated, if tragic, destiny of woman.

PROCTOR

Thomas Proctor wrote another of the poetical miscellanies
popular in the Elizabethan age. It was called *Gorgeous
Gallery of Gallant Inventions* (1578). In it, following the
traditional pattern, he invokes Penelope and Lucretia as
exemplary predecessors of the beautiful and virtuous "Mis-
tres D."[42]

GRANGE

The *Golden Aphroditis* is a curious work of John Grange,
a contemporary of Lyle, Pettie, and Shakespeare. Like Pettie,
he claims to have a feminine clientele in his reading public.
He culls at will from Tottel, Pettie, Golding, Erasmus, and
others. Though capable of a misogynistic mood, he sees his
own lady-love as an improved version of the best examples
of womanhood in classical lore. Polyxena, Penelope, Atalanta,
and Lucretia come to his mind. But his lady became more
exciting by association with the oriental pearl, the ruby,
and the cherry, then more exotic commodities than their
modern commercial counterparts. Chaucer had used the
ruby for the same type of comparison. In and after the fourteenth century it was used as a form of commendation. The
comparison of a lady with a pearl was a common compliment
in the romantic period of England, from Pettie to Herrick.

NASHE

With a kind of Juvenalian contempt for those who take to
the pen Thomas Nashe in his *Anatomie of Absurditie* (1589)
mentions Lucretia in the midst of an extensive confirmation
of woman's vices. Lucretia is the exception which proves

the rule. Ancient authors yielded for him an abundance of
historical and mythological examples of evil women. Writers
are roundly condemned who cater to the frivolity of the
times and seek to ingratiate themselves with women by
extolling their praises. Ovid's exile should be their warning.
With a ministerial gloominess he notes the lack of virtuous
precepts in this literature of indulgence. Lucretia's chaste
behavior stands out as a rare virtue amid woman's frailties.
Nashe unconsciously reveals how heavily the Renaissance
depended on classical antiquity in making its appraisal of
woman, and how distorted his thesis is in any unbiased
appraisal of either woman herself or her place in ancient
society.

SHAKESPEARE

The formative genetics of Shakespeare's *Lucrece* (1594)
have been thoroughly investigated.[43] In terms of the tradition
of the story and of an associative context they show him as
a working part of the tradition, not in revolt against it. Baldwin has wisely considered the sources of Shakespeare's story
in relation with books available to Shakespeare, and concludes that Ovid is the principal source. Shakespeare likens
Lucrece to a sleeping dove which has come under the observation of a night-owl, to an unsuspecting victim about to
be attacked by a lurking serpent (360-364), or to the prey
of a grim lion (421), or to a fowl marked by a falcon (506),
to mention a few of his comparisons. In relating the ominous
ravishing of Philomela by her brother-in-law, Tereus, Ovid
states that her sister Procne and Tereus were wedded under
the malign influence of the sacrilegious hoot-owl (*Metamorphoses* 6.431-433). He later likens Tereus to an eagle
which has caught a hare (516-518), and Philomela to a
lamb trapped by a wolf (527f.), and to a dove already the
victim of greedy claws (529f.). But in simple reticence Ovid
compared Lucretia with a small lamb caught by a deadly
wolf (*Fasti* 2.799f.).

Marsus' edition of Ovid's *Fasti* (Basle, 1550) supplied cor-
relative material, both Latin and Greek, in extensive notes.
Shakespeare could have obtained Livy's details and those of
Dionysius of Halicarnassus from Marsus. Both Livy's text
and Painter's translation of it also manifest themselves in
Shakespeare's poem. An edition of Livy appeared in Frank-
fort in 1568. Shakespeare's long poem (more than 1800 lines
in seven-line stanzas) is a composite of many sources and
influences. The standard dictionary of Shakespeare's day in
England was Cooper's *Thesaurus* (1565 and later editions),
and there is a borrowing from Cooper in the argument to the
Lucrece. The *Thesaurus* in turn was based upon Stephanus'
Dictionarium Historicum ac Poeticum, and Stephanus drew
partly from a work of Natalis Comes. There was no English
translation of the *Fasti* until 1640, after Shakespeare had died.
A topical statement of Publilius Syrus, a slave from Syria who
found a place of honor for himself in Rome in the time of
Augustus, invited elaboration (134-140). Memories of Vergil,
Horace, Juvenal, the Scriptures, Chaucer,[44] or Spenser may
haunt a given stanza. Rhetorical ornamentation, dramatization, copiousness, conceits, forensic pyrotechnics and an understandable attraction to the libido of a self-suppressing
nation which, still, was eager to acquaint itself with new
lights in the emotional spectrum, all get extensive play in the
poem. Sextus' approach to his sacrilegious deed Ovid encom-
passes in two lines, and Shakespeare in some 40 stanzas. One
line of Ovid Shakespeare elaborates in 16 stanzas. During the
period of *Lucrece* Shakespeare was writing *Richard III, Titus
Andronicus,* and *Romeo and Juliet.* Horror and pity were the
outer expressions of his absorption in an all-encompassing
evil.

Lucretia, like a frightened deer, debates within her own
soul the alternative of suicide—an attitude which assumes her
jurisdiction over her own problem and removes jurisdiction
from either the male relatives, which obtained in early Roman
legal procedure or from the Church doctrine, as noticed

earlier in St. Augustine's remarks. At first, Lucretia felt that
suicide would merely extend the pollution from the body to
the soul, like a mother who, having lost one baby, would kill
the other. Then in a series of analogies ranging from a pine
tree stripped of its bark, a sacked house, a spotted temple, and
a blemished fort she asks release from any charge of impiety
for the act, concluding

Tis honour to deprive dishonour'd life. (stanza 170)

A protestant indeed! The Renaissance heroine here re-thinks
her responsibilities. She does not neglect the authority of religion, but her final decision to conform with the tradition of
her legend comes from the analogies, which are probably
more British than mythological.[45]

Many stories were in vogue in the sixteenth century in
which the honor of a lady was subjected to pressure. A wife
of a soldier must choose whether to see her husband hanged
or to submit to one who controls her husband's fate. With a
compromise obviously not true to the early Roman version of
Lucretia's fate the husband pleaded with his wife to submit,
on the ground that when the mind does not consent, the body
is still unsoiled.[46] In *Measure for Measure* (1604) a sister
faces either compromise or the death of her brother, who
urges the former alternative upon his sister. She, however,
remains true to her own higher instincts.

The libretto of Puccini's *La Tosca* presents a similar plot,
laid in the early nineteenth century in Rome, a return to the
original locale. Scarpia, chief of police, subjects Cavaradossi
to torture in an attempt to discover the whereabouts of a political foe, Angelotti. Also, in an attempt to compel the lovely
Floria La Tosca to submit to his advances, he allows her to
listen to the agony of her lover Cavaradossi from the adjoining office. La Tosca has the choice of submission, or if she
refuses, the death of her lover. Cavaradossi begs her not to
reveal the hiding place of Angelotti. The original Lucretia
avoided death temporarily by submitting, in order to clear

her good name. La Tosca agrees to submit in order to save her lover. Meanwhile, however, in the office of Scarpia she found an instrument with which to kill him. But her attempt to flee in safety with Cavaradossi was frustrated, for the blank cartridges with which, by Scarpia's perfidious agreement, Cavaradossi was to be shot on the roof of the Castel San Angelo turned out to be real bullets, and La Tosca could escape the pursuing police only by jumping from the roof of the Castello.

The simultaneous appearance of Daniel's *Rosamund* (1592), of Shakespeare's *Venus and Adonis* (1593), and the popularity of his *Lucrece*, which went into a second edition in 1598, with others following in 1600, 1607, 1616, etc., reveal a literary following which was eager to confirm its hunger for sexual realism by reference to developed expressions of it in literature. Shakespeare also referred to Lucretia in *Twelfth Night*, *Taming of the Shrew*, and *Titus Andronicus*. In his time also Lucretia appeared on signet rings as a symbol of chastity.

HEYWOOD

Only months passed after the publication of Shakespeare's *Lucrece* until the probable appearance of Thomas Heywood's *The Rape of Lucrece*, a chronicle play broadly based on Livy's version, with a dramatization of the violation of Lucretia. Five editions of the play were published between 1608 and 1638. In it echoes have been found of Livy, Shakespeare's *Lucrece*, *Julius Caesar* (1599), and *Macbeth* (1606).

For the violation of Lucretia, Heywood relied upon Shakespeare's version. In imitation of the mob scene in the Roman Forum in *Julius Caesar* and following the same practice in early Renaissance painting Heywood used the corpse of Lucretia as a provocative force. An exuberant *farrago* of duels, murders, spectacle, elaborated sentiment, neatly turned couplets, Sunday school righteousness, banter and bawdy vulgarity, in a setting vacillating between that of the Forum and an English pub, the play at least catered to, if it did not serve,

the afternoon audience of Shakespeare's London. A drama-
tized version of the story, also based on Livy, was presented
at Strassburg in 1599, and may have been influenced by Heywood's play.[47]

MIDDLETON

Thomas Middleton published his *Ghost of Lucrece* (1600),
a continuation of the *Lucrece* of Shakespeare. The manuscript was discovered only in 1820. The ghost of Lucrece in a
tragic monologue laments her lost chastity. The Middle Ages
were slow to abandon their hold on her.

DONNE

John Donne in the early seventeenth century found the
appraisal of woman an engaging topic. An awareness of
woman's traditional inconstancy is aggravated by her delightful charm. It was a comfort, however, for him to realize that
some women were virtuous. Second thoughts led him to the
feeling that to make an issue of virginity is a vice, and that
"wife" is a better name than "virgin." A constant sense of
woman's responsibility is now accompanied by a growing
awareness of her capability.

CAREW

In the *Rapture* of the early twenties of the seventeenth century Thomas Carew, influenced by Jonson and Donne, gave
full expression to naturalism. Sheer exotic fabrics have obviously fed the fires of passion. Classical examples are revised
in order to endorse an Aristophanic abandon. Lucretia and
Penelope, the very symbols for centuries of uncompromised
chastity and conjugal fidelity, have become sybaritic in their
licentiousness in the Elysian Fields.

> The Roman Lucrece there reads the divine
> Lectures of Loves great master, Aretine.

Carew has here sacrilegiously associated Lucretia with the

knave and infidel Pietro Aretino (1492–1556), whose scurrilous and licentious pen held princes in fearful patronage.
He composed obscene sonnets for 16 engravings made by
Marcantonio Raimondi for the painter Giulio Romano. In his
Letters (1.310) Aretino criticizes Lucretia for the folly of
sacrificing her life for the principle of honor. He entitles his
letter "Down with honor, and long live shame." At this point
the story of Lucretia has found its other pole.

BURTON

The quality of the laughter of the laughing philosopher
Democritus of Abdera may be surmised by his self-styled
junior counterpart, Robert Burton (1577–1640), whose *Ana-
tomy of Melancholy* first appeared in 1621. In droll realism
unnecessary to reprint here Burton supplements Aretino's
sacrilegious defamation of Lucretia (III.II.I.II).

CASSONI

The Italian term *cassone* (pl.,*i*), originally denoting a large
marriage chest, came to include other pieces of household
furniture too. These articles were often painted with mythological, scriptural, and historical scenes which constitute an
important chapter in the cultural history of Italy from the
fourteenth to the sixteenth century. Tuscany and Umbria,
especially Florence, Siena, and Verona, were important centers of this work. Despite the demands made upon the time
of the masters of painting, they with their apprentices worked
extensively in this field, assuring to domestic articles of furniture, as was also true of the Greek ceramic art in its cultural setting, a place in the cultural development of a major
skill of the Renaissance. Signatures and dates are usually
lacking on *cassoni*. The painters of them followed the practice of their literary contemporaries in using subjects belonging in the remote past and treating them in the costumes and
customs of their contemporary society. The knowledge of
antiquity current in the early Renaissance and—more impor-

tant—the capacity of the period to project itself from its contemporary society into the more complex and developed
ancient society were so limited that it was easier for the artists
of the early Renaissance to translate a subject into contemporary *mores*. Not only was the setting then familiar, but also in
the content of the ancient story of Lucretia there were antici-
pations of their own interests: the observance and the violation of a code of hospitality, even within the bonds of kinship;
the violation and the satisfaction of a code of chivalry; the
practice of war as both an inducement to immorality and a
means of avenging it; and ancestral pride in the visible
remains of the Roman world in their own. In the later Renaissance artists were better equipped to recreate a subject in an
ancient setting, and were attracted to the more melodramatic
possibilities of this story and others. Since the ruse by which
Sextus forced Lucretia to submit was not carried out, it could
be more readily exploited in literature than in painting. Brutus
assumes an unusual prominence in the legend because of the
long tradition about him and his kin which pervaded Europe
in the Middle Ages.[48] Those who portrayed the story of Lucretia on *cassoni* drew from the *Gesta Romanorum,* Petrarch,
and behind them, from Livy and Ovid. Some representative
examples of the use of the story on *cassoni* will be given. The
locus classicus for *cassoni* is the monumental work of Schubring on the subject, and its supplement.[49]

An early Florentine chest of about the year 1400 portrays
the story of Lucretia in three scenes, as follows: 1) Tarquin
advances to the bed of Lucretia; 2) she stabs herself in the
presence of Brutus and Collatinus; 3) Tarquin the Proud and
the royal women are exiled from Rome, which is represented
behind a wall and gate by a campanile, a basilica, and a
domed building. The costuming is contemporary with the
chest.[50]

A *cassone* in Paris, of the school of Verona about the year
1430, bears a dramatic portrayal of the various phases of Lucretia's tragic fate. Sextus pulls away the covers from the nude

lady. Considerable care was taken with the portrayal of the bed and draperies, too. Before the bed a slave girl collapses on the floor, stabbed. Lucretia now dictates to her secretary the news of her shame. The sententious remark is recorded in Greek that it is better to die than to live in disgrace. Meanwhile, the guilty Sextus rides off to Rome. In the presence of Brutus, Collatinus, Spurius, and Valerius, and two groups of shocked friends, Lucretia takes her life.[51]

An interesting set of panels in Paris, of Florentine origin about 1460, tells this story in three parts. In the first part Sextus came to the house of Lucretia on horseback, and was hospitably received at the door of the palace by his intended victim. Through two windows of the house may be seen: a) Sextus and Lucretia sitting at table, and b) Sextus threatening the unclad lady in her bed. He then rides away. In the second part Lucretia in the dining hall of Brutus stabs herself among the shocked kin and friends. In the third part she lies in state in a shroud among two groups of mourners. Forming part of an architectural background are the Pantheon and the columns of Trajan and Marcus Aurelius! Professors of history are expected to close the book at this point. There will be other equally motivated opportunities later. In the portico of the Pantheon are young knights stunned by the tragedy. The painting is an interesting piece of pictorial realism. One is not only given access to the bedroom; but the lady is portrayed unclad. In time this phase of the story was exploited in the arts as it was in literature.[52]

Mrs. Gardner's Gallery in Boston has Sandro Botticelli's (1444–1510) panel of the story of Lucretia, made around 1500, perhaps for the house of Giovanni Vespucci. Of the three scenes on the panel, on the left Lucretia is fainting under the threat of Sextus at the entrance to the palace; and on the right she falls through a door into an open loggia in a state of collapse. In the center of the panel the corpse of the victim lies in state, surrounded by her armed kin and friends. In a funeral oration Brutus, standing at the base of a column, calls for revenge. The grim determination of the men about him contrasts with the shocked sense of pity expressed on the faces of the women. A formally balanced architectural setting for the scenes has been carefully worked out. Palaces, a free adaptation of the triumphal arch of Constantine, and a statue of the tyrannical David are deployed in and around an open piazza. Beyond, a Florentine gate and a landscape are visible. The buildings are adorned with bas-reliefs of historical events. The coloring effects add a subdued ominousness to the whole scene. The discreteness of the painting is in its detachment from the bedroom of Lucretia.[53]

But the dominant effect of this panel, one of the finest works of Botticelli, is its dramatic power. The violence and turbulence of life in Florence around the turn of the century, with the struggle of Lorenzo and Savonarola, lifted Botticelli's last years to a high level of emotional excitement. Great ideas, deepened by association with historical precedents, evoked corresponding dramatic action. The uncompromising heroism of Lucretia is allowed to assume its full measure of dramatic power and ideological significance.

Two earlier panels, one in the Pitti Gallery in Florence and the other in the Louvre in Paris, portraying the stories of Lucretia and Virginia respectively, bring to their subjects the same compelling seriousness. They are attributed to Filippino Lippi (1460–1505), the son of Fra Filippo Lippi. The father also was the early teacher of Botticelli. Thus, heroic subjects germinated in the mind of Botticelli, and reached their finest expression in him when historical events in Florence roused the painter to a high sense of ideological participation in them.

A panel in the Cluny Museum in Paris by Matteo di Giovanni portrays four phases of the story of Lucretia in a sequence. On the left Sextus has come to the ornate bedroom of his victim. The sword in Lucretia's hand indicates her determination not to survive her disgrace. In an open square before her palace Lucretia stands distracted in the presence of a servant girl. Brutus breaks the news of her death to Collatinus and his enraged companions. The two noblemen then ride to Rome to seek revenge. Considerable attention has been given to the architectural background. There is a triumphal arch and the Coliseum; on the gate of the city are the letters SPQR and a Roman eagle.[54]

Modena has a panel of Ercole Roberti portraying the suicide of Lucretia in the presence of Brutus and Collatinus in full armor. Lucretia is here dressed in the garb of a noble lady of Ferrara. The men bear expressions of regret on their faces, but they make no effort to prevent Lucretia from taking her life.[55]

A painting at Hannover of about the year 1505, the work of Sodoma (1477–1549), varies the tradition of Lucretia's death. Having left the estate of her husband, she took her life, alone on the banks of the Tiber. Against a background of a town perched on a mountain, a river, and bridge Lucretia plunged a sword in her bosom, laid bare. The picturesque scene reminds one of Vergil's lines:

> Tot congesta manu praeruptis oppida saxis
> fluminaque antiquas subter labentia muros.
> (*Georgics* 2.156f.)[56]

> So many towns hand-built upon rugged crags
> and rivers flowing under ancient walls.

There are two other paintings of Lucretia by Sodoma, one in the Royal Gallery in Turin and the other in Hamburg. Eurialo Morani d'Ascoli, a friend of Pietro Aretino and of Pope Leo X, wrote a poem about one of Sodoma's paintings of Lucretia.[57] Leo X, when still cardinal, wrote some Latin iambics on an ancient statue of Lucretia just then found in Rome. The fountain-head of this legend lies in the literary expressions of it. From these came a natural extension of the legend into the decorative arts. One of these expressions of the legend, in turn, after a millenium and a half, motivated a tribute in Latin verse. We here see the dynamic capacity of an old legend. Just as one movement of Mahler's Seventh Symphony

Lucretia. Engraving by Marcantonio Raimondi. National Gallery
(Corsini), Rome

Death of Lucretia. Faenza Bowl, Victoria and Albert Museum, London

is said to have been inspired by Rembrandt's *Night Watch,*
and another by the poetry of Eichendorff.

A *cassone* in Venice has on it a different sequence of scenes
from those heretofore recognized. They are grouped into two
pictures. In the first picture Sextus, in full armor, accosts Lucretia at her bed. On the arrival of her kin she takes her life
in bed. The men make no effort to prevent the suicide; in
fact, most of them, under emotional stress, have their backs
turned on her. Her corpse lies in state among mourning
women and armed men. Renaissance palaces and a round
domed building form an architectural background for the
scenes. In the second picture Brutus and Collatinus hold
council with their comrades at a table. The setting is a camp
with armed forces. They then prepare to depart.[58]

The influence on cassoni of Petrarch's *Triumphs* is easily
found. Both Petrarch and the painters used Lucretia as an
example of allegorized qualities such as Renown, Chastity,
and the like.[59]

OTHER PAINTINGS

Paintings on the story of Lucretia are generally devoted to
the suicide. This, despite the Christian strictures on the subject, still illustrates the fulfillment of heroic resolve.

Bramantino, whose flourishing period was in the early sixteenth century, painted an admirable clothed Lucretia, which
is now in Milan. She is portrayed as taking her own life in a
context which is not without its Christian implications. For
Lucretia's outstretched arms are centered by the vertical
lines of a column in a classical building, and in the background a lady, distracted by the tragedy which she observes,
stands as though petrified, with arms outstretched, cruciform.
A formal colonnade provides an architectural background.[60]
In the Johnson Collection in Philadelphia there is also a
Lucretia of Bramantino.[61]

Titian (1477–1576) painted a *Tarquin and Lucretia,* now
in the Wallace Collection in England. He has another in

Vienna. Giorgione (1477–1510) portrayed Brutus in the act of swearing revenge before Lucretia and Tarquin,[62] and, in another painting, Lucretia revealing to Brutus the insult inflicted on her by Tarquin. The National Gallery in London has the *Lucretia* of Lorenzo Lotto, who was a contemporary of Titian and Giorgione in Venice in the early sixteenth century. A lady with beribboned turban, low-cut dress, and elaborate pendant hanging from it stands brooding between a chair and a table. In her left hand she holds a drawing of a nude Lucretia about to stab herself, to which she points. On the table lies a bouquet of flowers and a piece of paper bearing a quotation from Livy:

> Nec ulla impudica Lucretiae exemplo vivet.

> Nor shall any lady live in immodesty by the example of Lucretia.

This is one of Lorenzo Lotto's most colorful pictures. His interest in woman's lapse from chastity is revealed in his painting in the Louvre[63]—common also in the period—*Christ and the Adulteress.*

One Lucretia of Palma Vecchio is in the Borghese Gallery in Rome and another is in Vienna. These paintings belong to the period 1517–1525. Both are half-length portraits of a clothed lady about to take her life. In the version in Vienna a man behind her puts his hand on her left arm.[64]

One must be satisfied with a vicarious approach to the *Lucretia* of Parmigianino of the early sixteenth century. This painting was lost, but it left behind a tradition as a *cosa divina.* The closest approach to it is probably in drawings in Budapest from the artist's own hand. One of these, in turn, owes something to the print of Marcantonio Raimondi inspired by Raphael's *Lucretia.* The cross-fertilizing of influence is here apparent. An engraving by Enea Vico is another way of approaching the original *Lucretia* of Parmigianino. It portrays a nude woman, sword in hand, sitting on a bed. The *Lucretia* in Naples, sometimes attributed to Parmigianino, at least seems to bear some indebtedness to his lost painting.[65]

The Borghese Gallery in Rome has a *Lucretia* of Pontormo, a young protégé of Leonardo da Vinci, Piero di Cosimo, and Andrea del Sarto. Its date is slightly earlier than 1530. It is a bust of the young girl, who has one breast bared and wears a gilded bronze headdress. In one hand she holds upright a bronze-handled dagger.[66]

The Walters Art Gallery in Baltimore has a vellum manuscript of the middle of the sixteenth century which portrays illustrious persons. Lucretia and Regulus are among them. She is the only lady in this assemblage, which ranges from Themistocles to Erasmus.[67]

Tintoretto, of the Venetian School, was attracted to the legend of Lucretia early in the second half of the sixteenth century. One of his versions of the violation is in Madrid, and another in a private collection in New York. The latter version is one of his most dramatic compositions on a profane subject. Tarquin is portrayed as seizing from behind a partially veiled Lucretia. In the confusion one of the statues holding the draperies has been overturned. Pearls are seen dropping from Lucretia's broken necklace. At her feet lies Tarquin's sword. The painter's concern over the moral problem may be inferred from his several scriptural paintings of adulterous women. Tintoretto, sometimes known as "Il Furioso," gave continuity to the noble tradition of Michelangelo and Titian.[68]

Veronese's (1528–1588) *Death of Lucretia,* in Vienna, presents a clothed Lucretia in the act of stabbing herself. She is heavily adorned with bracelets, rings, and necklaces. Veronese, too, painted a biblical version of an adulterous woman.[69]

A vellum manuscript of the seventeenth century, in the Vatican Library, Gaudenzi Paganini's *Dissertationes rerum politicarum et moralium,* contains an illustration (*folio* 243) of Lucretia in the act of destroying herself.[70]

The Genoese painter Luca Cambiaso (1527–1585) made two versions of the suicide of Lucretia: one dated around 1575 and now in a private collection in Lugano, and the other in the Prado Gallery in Madrid. She is portrayed as stabbing herself in the breast while standing beside her couch. The painting in Lugano, a sketch of which is also extant, served as a model for Guido Reni's version of the death of Cleopatra, now in the Ventura collection in Florence.[71] In the Brera Palace in Milan there is a fine drawing of Lucretia in the same pose as the previously mentioned paintings of Cambiaso.

Guido Reni (1572–1642) of Bologna made three paintings of Lucretia's self-sacrifice. His *Lucretia*, in Potsdam, of about 1625, in keeping with the style of its period is a melodramatic painting. With her sensual, white body, one breast bare, lighted against a dark background and accentuated by exquisitely beautiful drapery and an elegant setting, Lucretia stands poised before a couch, sword in hand, ready to inflict upon herself the fatal blow. On the floor lies the sheath of the sword.[72] Another *Lucretia* of his, on wood, is in Rome. The young woman, with a sweet langour touching the despair and pathos on her face, a delightful half-nude, is not unworthy to be a Venus. She reclines on a couch, dagger in hand.[73]

The Capitoline Gallery in Rome has another *Lucretia* of Guido Reni. This painting, from the last years of the artist, is a significant portrayal of the ancient Roman heroine. The artist's sentimental attachment to his national origins enabled him to recapture the intense emotional climate in which the tragedy must have originally taken place. With her breast bared, Lucretia is about to stab herself. She visibly bears the uncompromising ideal which created the moral issue in the violation, and the melancholy of her passion and grief. Her only comfort is that of the caressing night, with eerie silvery moonlight filtering through to her from afar, like the strains of a distant melody.[74]

The beautiful new Capodimonte Gallery in Naples has several portrayals of Lucretia, the most notable probably being that of Luca Giordano (1634–1705).

At Narford, in England, there is *The Death of Lucretia* of Pellegrini (1675–1741). A Venetian, Pellegrini was the first of

the Italian painters to arrive in England at the opening of the
eighteenth century, the beginning of the Italianizing influence
on English painting.[75]

The National Gallery of Art in Washington has Giuseppe
Crespi's (1665–1747) *Lucretia Threatened by Tarquin.* The
clothed lady struggles for her honor before her couch.[76]

Lucas Cranach (1472–1553), an acquaintance of Martin
Luther, painted in Germany an amazing variety of Lucretias
within a narrow range of expression, over two decades in the
first half of the sixteenth century. He usually painted a thinly
veiled and partially nude Lucretia, adorned with jewelry, and
in the act of taking her own life. He amply did his part to
inculcate in women of his time and place the need of fidelity
in wedlock, and in men reasons for violating such resolutions
on the part of women. Views of the Rhineland with castles on
crags are provided for background. His paintings are sometimes touched with a bizarre, humorous realism. One of his
Lucretias wears a large modish hat and hair net. She has
pulled the black robe from the front of her body in order to
destroy herself. Some of his figures are life-size and some are
half figures. His Lucretias may be found all over Europe and
in the United States.[77]

Albrecht Dürer (1471–1528) in a sense represents the classical tradition in reverse. Although his first visit to Italy is
said to be the beginning of the Renaissance in northern
Europe, his skill greatly influenced the classical tradition in
the land whence he derived his inspiration. At Nuremberg
there is a Lucretia of Dürer, done in his most exacting crafts-
manship.[78] In Munich there is another Lucretia of his, belonging to the early sixteenth century.[79] In Vienna there is a drawing of Lucretia used in the painting in Munich. Here again
there is an enrichment in the cross-fertilizing of skills.

Dutch painters, too, expressed themselves through this
story. Joos van Cleve, the Elder *(fl.* 1511–1541), has a Lucretia in Vienna and one in San Francisco. Cornelis Cornelisz
(1493–1544) painted a half-nude-standing Lucretia in the

act of stabbing herself, now in Berlin. It shows the influence
of the celebrated Lucretia of Marcantonio Raimondi. Other
Lucretias were painted by Hendrick Goltzius, Jan Gossaert,
and Geeraert van der Meiri.[80]

Rembrandt (1606–1669) was one of the many Dutch
painters whose work carried the story of Lucretia into northern Europe and, in time, widely over the Western World. He
was one of the few who failed to succumb to the spell of Italy.
Several paintings of Lucretia came from his hand. One of his
Lucretias (1664) is heavily adorned with pearl necklace, a
medallion with a pearl hanging on her breast, pearls in her
ears, and a golden diadem on her head. With a gesture of
despair Lucretia puts the dagger to her breast.[81] Another admirable Lucretia of his is a genuine Dutch heroine with pain
and pallor on her features.[82]

ENGRAVING, WOODCUTS

The new-born art of engraving and woodcuts, brought to
a new peak of eminence by Dürer's graphic skill, enabled the
artist to reach the world with pictures in an extensive way.
For a century the influence of Dürer's work was felt in prints,
painting, sculpture, enamels, tapestry, and other arts, from
Spain to Russia. Dürer learned his classical lore informally.

The golden age of woodcuts in Florence was in the *Quattrocento*. Stories are told through this art with a childlike sim-
plicity, as was true of the cassoni, too. An Italian manuscript
in the British Museum of the fifteenth century, the story of
Lucretia, contains a vivid and dramatic woodcut of Lucretia
clothed and standing proudly upright as she plunges the
dagger into her bosom. Her kinsmen are seated around a
table, transfixed with terror. An overturned stool confirms
the violence of the scene.[83]

Marcantonio Raimondi, born in Bologna about 1480,
became the chief Italian master of engraving, under the influence of his contemporaries, Albrecht Dürer and Raphael.
His earliest dated print is of the year 1505. His chief activity

—possibly to the misfortune of his craft—was to copy the works of other artists. His *Lucretia*, originating with Raphael, was a masterpiece in its own right which delighted the master of painting and was followed by a close attachment and collaboration of the two artists lasting several years. This Lucretia, which caught the inner spirit of the original, is full-length and draped, with one breast bared for the mortal blow. The graceful poise and rhythm of the tragic figure, the flowing drapery, the emotional strain, and the harmonizing of human figure with the architectural background are all done with an easy felicity, as if by a rebirth of Attic sophistication. An inscription in Greek in the left corner says that it is preferable to die rather than to live shamefully. This *Lucretia* of Raimondi is in the National Gallery (Corsini) in Rome.[84] A *Lucretia* of Jacopo Francia, an understudy of Marcantonio Raimondi, is in the British Museum. It shows obvious dependence on the works of the master.[85]

A Dutch artist Lucas van Leyden made a woodcut of the nude Lucretia, with hair cascading to her waist, putting the sword to her bosom. The date of the woodcut is 1514.[86] A woodcut of Giuseppe Porta-Salviati dated in the year 1553 portrays Lucretia, book in hand, and her attendant ladies working with their wool, as her husband's group of soldiers enters the room behind them.[87]

The French designer of illustrated books Gravelot made a Lucretia in 1768.

The English poet William Blake (1757–1827) brought to his craft of drawing a great technical skill, an Olympian grandeur, and exalted imagination. In his lofty concept of the artist's mission great art was to keep alive the eternal beauty in time and circumstance. For a new edition of Charles Allen's *Roman History* (1798) Blake made four copper plates, one of them the *Death of Lucretia*. It is a fortunate textbook which can boast of this quality in its illustrative material. Lucretia is also found on monograms of the sixteenth and seventeenth centuries.[88]

TAPESTRY

Lucretia's tragic story also found expression, as would be expected, in tapestry throughout Europe. The courtly traditions of the late Middle Ages brought with them a romantic exaltation of woman. Lucretia demonstrated that woman could be not only heroic, but in her heroism, beautiful. Those who could not read were able to understand through pictures. Among Petrarch's series of triumphs there was the *Triumph of Fame,* in which Lucretia appropriately appeared. She was among the few women so recognized, and the only Roman heroine among them. From this document she made her way into tapestry, as well as into the other arts.[89] It is not difficult to confirm the popularity of this old Roman story in European art. Many able artists provided the designs for such tapestries. As examples, we know that Francesco Salviati (1510–1563) of Florence, a painter of some renown, provided the cartoons for a review of the story of Lucretia, and that in the inventory of Daniel Fourment in the year 1643, in Antwerp, there were 12 pieces on the story of Tarquin the Proud and Lucretia.[90]

OPERA

The story of Lucretia has found expression twice in opera. Kaspar Schweizelsperg, a German composer of Bavaria, wrote an opera in German, *Die romanische Lucretia* (1714), with a prologue and three acts. It is his only opera extant. The identity of the librettist is unknown. The opera was performed at Durlach, Coburg, and Nuremburg. A detailed description of the opera was made in recent times by the man who then owned the score, and printed parts of the overture have been found.

In 1937 a one-act opera was performed in Italian at La Scala in Milan, called *Lucrezia.* The score was written by Respighi of Bologna, to whose music all lovers of Rome are indebted, and the libretto is by Guastalla. The opera was later performed in Buenos Aires and Rio de Janeiro. A Czech

text has also been used in the performance of the opera. The
opera resembles a seventeenth-century dramatic recitative.[51]

POTTERY

Lucretia also found her way into European pottery. On a
tile painted in colors Lucretia, wearing a curious headdress,
takes her life. She makes the same gesture as is seen in the
approximately contemporary *Lucretia* of Lucas Cranach in
Munich. This piece of majolica derived from the Netherlands.[92] A majolica plate in the Civic Museum in Bologna
depicts the death of Lucretia. Its maker, called the Lucretia-
painter for want of better identification, takes his name from
the plate.[93] A majolica bowl of about the year 1530 in the
Victoria and Albert Museum in London (#797) shows
Lucretia, with breast bared, stabbing herself. The treatment
shows an indebtedness to Marcantonio Raimondi and, behind
him, to Raphael. An inscription written in Greek on the balus-
trade of the colonnade in which she stands says, "Better to
die than to live ignobly." In the background there is a river
crossed by a bridge, and several buildings and mountains.[94]
Lucretia's suicide is portrayed on two majolica plates in the
Bargello in Florence.

Lucretia is also found portrayed on one panel of a tankard
of German origin of about the year 1576.[95] And on a lead-
glazed piece of earthenware possibly made for Wedgwood
about 1800 Lucretia, unclad, sleeps on a couch adorned with
flowered drapery and a yellow cushion.[96]

Thus an ancient legend has found expression in a late phase
of one of the oldest of the arts. The Italian potters of the
Renaissance responded to historical forces and technological
achievements which began with Marco Polo in the Far East
and with the Crusades in the Near East. Chinese, Byzantine,
and Islamic impulses brought new expressions to classical
experience. The old Roman town of Faenza some 30 miles
southeast of Bologna gave its name to a distinctive kind of
glazed and painted earthenware. The masters of this craft,

when dispersed from Faenza, carried on their work in Siena and elsewhere. Porcelain introduced from the East and majolica developed in the West were exciting new carriers of ancient experience, and new forces in an expanding and competitive economy in Italy of the time.

REVIEW

The recorded story of Lucretia's tragic fate began with "Livy's pictured page." With a narrative skill intense with unforgettable fire and color within its few lines Livy fused from documents, when available, and imagination when not, a poetically touched and romantically conceived legend of early Roman history which may never have happened in quite that way, but which, nevertheless, caught the authentic spirit of a heroic lady who deserved not to remain unsung. His story is a spark from a fire, not a smudge. Its warmth was to be felt in various ways through the long history of two Roman civilizations, pagan and Christian.

The sanctity of the chastity of woman is a natural expression of a patriarchal society. In Rome laws soon came into being to punish violations of the sanctity of wedlock and the home. The coming of eloquence to the story was inevitable, if not very significant. Ovid has retold the story with a lively sense of the irresistible charm of a chaste young woman. Never is he more vivacious than in describing the seduction of a lovely young blonde whose artless innocence is her undoing. His tongue-in-cheek wit received short rope amid the flat, early-Christian vituperations of sex. But the heroic attachment of Lucretia to principle, in the face of death, brought comfort and courage to other women whom first the tyranny of the Empire and later the invasions of the barbarian brought to the same dilemma.

St. Augustine felt constrained to discountenance suicide, even under the circumstances of the story. His religious devoutness lifted him above the world, but he was still a realist in it. An allegorical interpretation of the story is found in

the *Gesta Romanorum*. To search for hidden meanings is
often to be blind to the obvious ones. The Middle Ages were
generally contemptuous of woman and sex, but in their later
phase the best minds, out of abundant evidence of woman's
innate virtues, invested her not only with her first oriental
luxuries, but also with spiritual sublimity. The glorification of
Lucretia by Petrarch and Boccaccio deeply influenced for
centuries European thought and the arts born of it. The story
also supported a Herodotean cyclical philosophy in a work
of Boccaccio, with its implication of the need for restraint
in the presence of woman.

The early English writers approached the story of Lucretia's violation with eloquence, a conscience, and a natural
hunger to open new doors of experience. They rejected the
Continental cynicism felt for women. In an increasingly
secular and indulging world the story invited restatement,
elaboration, and imaginative adornment. Especially in an
environment of narrow dimensions in living the story brought
a natural—if violent—release into emotional and spiritual
expression again. There was also the responsibility of woman
to her own conscience and society. Since the cultural experience of the West has been transmitted largely by men and
through men, they, unless entirely immune to the experience
they created, must have felt the constant impulse to respond
properly to the social problem presented by the story. It is
undeniably true, aside from the last two generations, that
the great literature of the world has affirmed faith in the
integrity, goodness, and promise of human nature. The great
who have come to this story have fluoroscopically revealed
in it the nobility of the human spirit.

There have been times when the moral earnestness of one
period created a responsive note in that of another; at other
times the impulse to narrate, through the media of the various
arts, led artists to make important interpretations in their own
crafts. For them and their times the story was educational,
as it brought to life appetite and excitement under the form

of high purpose. Later artists were drawn to the suicide, to the dramatic, or even the melodramatic, phase of the story. It gave them a chance to create a beautiful woman in her hour of extreme distress, and to decide on the costuming or lack of it, the expression of the mood, and details of the background. Increasing attention to the charms and adornments of the violated lady encouraged the very act which the story professed to condemn, and continued to remind women of the burden of responsibility laid on them, in another time and possibly in their own, even under uncontrollable circumcumstances.

By the seventeenth century the story seems to have lost its drive. Perhaps all that could be said had been said. Shakespeare's *Lucrece* leaves little more to be said, short of abandoning the whole structure of value which the story assumed at the outset—the problematical contribution to the story made by Carew and Burton. The story had carried man through to the point where he was simply delighting in a full expression of natural eroticism. The maturing of European society and a developed judicial system eliminated suicide as woman's recourse in an act of injustice. Such an extreme form of self-imposed penalty must have come to seem disparate with the possible delinquence in the eyes of both the victim and society, especially in times of general historical turbulence, when women were regarded as part of the fruits of victory.

In stimulating artistic expression the legend played its part in the growth of European economy, which, because non-mechanized, relied upon the arts. The mobility of artists and their works, the demand for their creations as useful, beautiful, and meaningful products, provided constructive channels of communication in not only the arts, but social relations as well. From one art another was cross-fertilized, and since the legend bore value by responsible choice in a context of feminine beauty, both arts, hearts, and minds were exposed to the civilizing effects of the legend.

> For men are changed by what they do.
>   W. H. Auden

A review of the iconological evidence pertaining to the legend brings to clearer focus the vitality, the continuity, and the pervasiveness of classical antiquity in the later history of the West.

Under the influence of the legend an imposing body of evidence grew up in time which suggested the emergence of the universal from the particular—of the common bond of humanity through the diversities of time, space, faith, and circumstance. If the energy of the legend was finally spent, it had lent its strength to useful purposes, artistic and social. A heroic woman, acting from a self-imposed resolve of absolute integrity, was a constant reminder to women, as the original Lucretia had observed, of their responsibility to themselves and society, but also a reminder to men of their responsibility. In response to her tragic plight society has generally provided for Lucretia firm laws and a mature social climate. In its final effect the cultural tradition of the legend confirms the alliance of conscience with consciousness in the Helleno-Roman-Judaio-Christian heritage.

Notes

THE STORY OF CYRUS THE GREAT, pp. 1 to 58

1 A. H. Krappe, "Le mythe de la naissance de Cyrus," in *Revue des études grecques* 43 (1930), 153.
2 Robert Byron, *The Road to Oxiana* (London, Lehmann, 1950), 169.
3 Aemilius Baehrens, *Poetae Latini Minores* (Leipzig, Teubner, 1883), vol. 5: 402 (#3) and 403 (#4).
4 George G. Cameron, "The Monument of King Darius at Bisitun," *Archaeology* 13.3 (1960), 162-171; and C. W. Ceram, *The March of Archaeology* (New York, Knopf, 1958), 204-208.
5 *True History*, introduction to book 1.
6 R. Henry, *Ctésias* (Brussels, Lebègue, 1947), 12f. (Bekker, 36a).
7 *Ibid.*, 15f. (Bekker, 36b).
8 *Ibid.*, 17 (Bekker, 36b-37a); Photius 2.6.8.
9 *Ibid.*, 18 (Bekker, 37a).
10 C. Müller, *Fragmenta Historicorum Graecorum* (Paris, Didot, 1848), 2.91 (#10).
11 Migne, *Patrologiae Cursus Completus*, vol. 27, column 375.
12 Theodor Mommsen, *Iordanis Romana et Getica* (Berlin, Weidmann, 1882) in *Monumenta Germaniae Historica* vol. 5, part 1, *Romana*, p. 8, line 5.
13 Athenaeus 14.633 c-e in *F. H. G.* (see note 10), 2.90f. (#7).
13a Cicero, ad *Quintum*, 1.1.8.
14 Henry, *op. cit.* (see note 6), 12f. (Bekker 36a).
15 *F. H. G.* (see note 10), vol. 3, fragment 66 (pp. 397-406).
16 Henry W. Litchfield, "National *Exempla Virtutis* in Roman Literature," in *Harvard Studies in Classical Philology* 25 (1914), 1-71.
17 Cf. also his work *Against Apion* 1: 132, 145, 154.
18 Migne, *op. cit.*, (see note 11), vol. 24, col. 457.
19 *Ibid.*, sections 531, 532 in col. 456, 457.
20 Mommsen, *op. cit.* (see note 12), *Romana*, p. 8, section 58.

21 Migne, *op. cit.* (see note 11), vol. 181: in commentary on *Isaiah,* col. 428, verse 28.

22 Trenchard Cox, *Jehan Foucquet* (London, Faber, 1931), plate 46.

23 In his *True History* (2.17) Lucian finds the two Cyruses in the Elysian Plain on the Island of the Blest. There Alexander the Great was assigned a seat next to Cyrus the Great (2.9).

24 Gordon, *op. cit.* (see note 19 in chapter 2), 206.

25 De Laborde, *op. cit.* (see note 11 in chapter 2), 2.434.

26 *Ibid.,* 2.458.

27 Migne, *op. cit.* (see note 11) vol. 16, col. 1023 (epistle 18), 841.36.

28 *Ibid.,* vol. 69, col. 1259, chap. 10.; and C. C. Mierow, *The Gothic History of Jordanes* (Princeton, University Press, 1915).

29 Migne, *op. cit.* (see note 11), vol. 69, col. 1259, chap. 10c.

30 Manitius, *op. cit.* (see note 18 in chapter 2), 227.

31 Max Manitius, *Geschichte der Lateinischen Literatur des Mittelalters* (Munich, Beck, 1931), 156-159.

32 Migne, *op. cit.* (see note 11), vol. 198, col. 1470f. *(Book of Daniel,* chap. 16).

33 To complicate matters the Migne text capitalizes *canem,* transferring the word into the name of a person, the wife of the shepherd.

34 Both St. Jerome before him and Hervaeus, another commentator on the Scriptures, after him concurred in this piece of popular etymologizing.

35 #88, p. 416, ed. Oesterley.

36 Utley, *op. cit.* (see note 29 in chapter 2), #46 and 236.

37 Part 1, chap. 17.

38 Fritz Saxl and Hans Meier, *Catalogue of Astrological and Mythological Illuminated Manuscripts of the Latin Middle Ages,* vol. 3, part 1 *(Manuscripts in English Libraries,* London, Warburg Institute, 1953), 62f. (additional Ms. 20698).

39 *Ibid.,* 71 for such a manuscript (additional Ms. 25884) in the British Museum, of the late 14th century, with illuminated miniatures.

40 J. van den Gheyn, *Christine de Pisan, Epître d'Othéa à Hector,* arranged by Jean Miélot (Brussels, Vromant, 1913), #57 (folio 6ov.).

41 Paul O. Kristeller, *Medieval and Renaissance Latin Translations and Commentaries* (Washington, Catholic University of America, 1960).

42 Stornajolo, *op. cit.* (see note 50), #151, fol. 348 (p. 290).

43 Ioannes Mercati, *Codices Vaticani Graeci,* vol. 1 (Rome, Vatican, 1923), #122 and 123 (p. 153).

44 Montague R. James, *The Western Manuscripts in the Library of Trinity College, Cambridge* (Cambridge, University Press, 1901), vol. 2, #820.13 (p. 260); and vol. 3 (1902), #1304.9 (p. 325).

45 Montague R. James, *op. cit.* (see note 17 in chap. 2), #169.22, *fol.* 43 (p. 375).

46 *Ibid.*, #169.23, *fol.* 44 (p. 375).

47 Konrad Escher, *Die Miniaturen in den Basler Bibliotheken, Museen und Archiven* (Basel, Kober, 1917), #151, *fol.* 93, plate 31.1.

48 James, *op. cit.* (see note 17 in chap. 2), #203.6 (p. 405).

49 Utley, *op. cit.* (see note 29 in chap. 2), #247 (p. 224).

50 Cosimus Stornajolo, *Codices Urbinates Graeci Bibliothecae Vaticanae* (Rome, Vatican, 1895), #107 (pp. 163-166).

51 Garden City, New York, Doubleday.

52 Stornajolo, *op. cit.* (see note 50), 163.

53 Saxl and Meier, *op. cit.* (see note 38), 156. The miniatures of Lucretia in this manuscript (Harl. 1766) are noted on p. 95 of chap. 2. For other miniatures on Lucretia consult Walter De Gray Birch, *Early Drawings and Illuminations in the British Museum* (London, Bagster, 1879).

54 *Ibid.*, 80 (miniature of additional Ms. 35321). See Sir Edward M. Thompson, "The Rothschild Ms. in the British Museum of *Les cas des malheureux nobles hommes et femmes,*" *Burlington Magazine* 7 (1905), 198-210.

55 George M. Richter, *Andrea dal Castagno* (University of Chicago Press, 1943), 17 and plates 42 and 43.

56 Schubring, *op. cit.* (see note 49 in chap. 2), 202.

57 Edward Dillon, *Rubens* (London, Methuen, 1909), plates 300 and 342.

58 Georges Pascal, *Largillierre* (Paris, Beaux-Arts, 1928), #215 (p. 78) and plate 32.

59 M. Louis Dimier, *Les peintres français du xviiie siècle* (Paris, Van Oest, 1930), vol. 2: 258f. and 262f.

60 Göbel, *op. cit.* (see note 89 in chap. 2), vol. 1, part 1,68.

61 E. S. Siple, "Some Recently Identified Tapestries in the Gardner Museum in Boston," *Burlington Magazine* 57 (second part), (1930), 236-242. Plates 2A and 2B represent topics #1 and #3 respectively.

62 Göbel, *op. cit.* (see note 89 in chap. 2), 1.1.327. See also
   1.1.368; 2.1.475 and 569; 3.2 (Berlin, Brandus, 1934): 20,
   30, 272 (#38); and Albert F. Calvert, *The Spanish Royal
   Tapestries* (New York, John Lane, 1921), 62-64 and plates
   99-109.

63 Göbel, *op. cit.* (see note 89 in chap. 2), vol. 1, part 2, plate 279.

64 *Ibid.*, 1,1,196f.

65 *Ibid.*, 2,1,527.

66 *Ibid.*, 1,1,198.

67 G. L. Hunter, *The Practical Book of Tapestries* (Philadelphia,
   J. B. Lippincott Co., 1925), 154 and 157.

68 Göbel, *op. cit.* (see note 89 in chap. 2), 1,1,376.

69 Denucé, *op. cit.* (see note 90 in chap. 2), Vol. 4: 118, 122,
   139, 169, 183, 188, and 264. Panthea's name in the records has
   become "Pantena" or a close variant.

70 Göbel, *op. cit.* (see note 89 in chap. 2), 2,1,569; 2,2: illustration 492.

71 *Ibid.*, 1,1,379.

72 Hunter, *op. cit.* (see note 67), 226.

THE STORY OF LUCRETIA, pp. 59 to 125

1 Hans Galinsky, *Der Lucretia-Stoff in der Weltliteratur* (Breslau,
   Priebatsch, 1932).

2 Texts of Roman law regarding adultery may be found in Jo-
   hannes Baviera, *Fontes Iuris Romani ante-Iustiniani* (Florence,
   Barbèra, 1940), II 552-556.

3 J. G. Frazer, *Psyche's Task* (London, Macmillan, 1920), index
   under "adultery."

4 *Obsidione*, Livy 1.57.3 and Ovid, *Fasti* 2.722; *certamine*,
   L. 1.57.7 and *certamina*, *Fasti* 2.731; *suam quisque laudare*,
   L. 1.57.6 and *quisque suam laudat*, *Fasti* 2.731; *verbis opus
   esse*, L. 1.57.7 and *non opus est verbis*, *Fasti* 2.734; *regias
   nurus*, L. 1.57.9 and *nurus regis*, *Fasti* 2.739; *precibus minas*,
   L. 1.58.3 and *precibus . . . minisque*, *Fasti* 2.805; *hostis pro
   hospite*, L. 1.58.8 and *hostis ut hospes*, *Fasti* 2.787; *dedecus*,
   L. 1.58.4 and *Fasti* 2.826; *coacta*, L. 1.58.9 and *coacto*, *Fasti*
   2.829; *stirpe*, L. 1.59.1 and *Fasti* 2.843.

5 Ruth Kelso, *Doctrine for the Lady of the Renaissance* (Urbana, University of Illinois Press, 1956), 24-30.

6 Blum and Lauer, *op. cit.* (see note 20), plate 47.

7 1.1.7 (Teubner text, p. 13); 1.3.9 (Teubner, pp. 15f.); and 1.17.24 (Teubner, p. 39).

8 Migne, *Patrologiae Cursus Completus,* vol. 2 (Paris, 1878), section 929 (p. 978) and section 952 (p. 1003).

9 Migne, vol. 1, section 625 (pp. 698f.).

10 Migne, vol. 27, p. 377.

11 A. De Laborde, *Les manuscrits à peintures de La Cité de Dieu de Saint Augustin* (Paris, Rahir, 1909, 2 vol.), 2.430.

12 Carol Zangemeister, text of Orosius in *Corpus Scriptorum Ecclesiasticorum Latinorum* (Vienna, 1882), xxv.

13 1.7.11 (Teubner, p. 14).

14 Theodor Mommsen, *Iordanis Romana et Getica* in *Monumenta Germaniae Historica* (Berlin, Weidmann, 1882), vol. 5, part 1, p. 13, lines 22-25, and p. 14, lines 17f.

15 Frederick Tupper and Marbury B. Ogle, *Master Walter Map's Book* (London, Chatto and Windus, 1924), 132, 186.

16 *A Bibliography of the Survival of the Classics* (Warburg Institute, London, 1938, 2 vol.), 2.220f. (#836).

17 Montague R. James, *A Descriptive Catalogue of the Manuscripts in the Fitzwilliam Museum* (Cambridge, University Press, 1895) 373 (Ms. #169.25).

18 Max Manitius, *Handschriften antiker Autoren in Mittelalterlichen Bibliothekskatalogen* (Leipzig, Harrassowitz, 1935), 73-76.

19 D. J. Gordon, *Fritz Saxl* (London, Nelson, 1957), 205f. in "The Latin Classics Known to Boston of Bury," by R. A. Mynors.

20 André Blum and Philippe Lauer, *La miniature française aux xve et xvie siècles* (Paris, Van Oest, 1930), plate 57. (Fr. 273, 274).

21 G. Billanovich, "Petrarch and the Textual Tradition of Livy," in the *Journal of the Warburg and Courtauld Institutes* 14 (1951), 137-208.

22 F. Neri, *Francesco Petrarca* (Milan, Ricciardi, 1951).

23 Blum and Lauer, *op. cit.* (see note 20), plate 75.

24 Nicola Festa, *Francesco Petrarca, L'Africa* (Florence, Sansoni, 1926).

25 Arthur M. Young, *Legend Builders of the West* (University of Pittsburgh Press, 1958), 90.

26 Identical parts of the two texts are noted, as follows:

Livy	Boccaccio
regii iuvenes	*regiis iuvenibus*
suam quisque	*suam . . . unus quisque*
conscendimus equos	*conscensis . . . equis*
incaluerant vino	*calentibus vino*
citatis equis	*c(ita)tis equis*
cum aequalibus	*inter aequales*
benigne	*benigne*
per vim	*per vim*
sopitique omnes	*omnes sopitos*
gladio	*gladio*
si emiseris vocem	*si vocem emitteret*
"Ego me etsi peccato absolvo	*"Ego me, si peccato absolvo*
supplicio non libero; nec ulla	*supplicio non libero, nec ulla*
deinde inpudica Lucretiae	*deinceps impudica Lucrecie*
exemplo vivet."	*vivet exemplo."*
moribunda	*moribunda*
cultrum, quem sub veste	*cultrum quem sub veste*
abditum	*texerat*

27 Cf. Vitam cum sanguine fudit, Ovid, *Metamorphoses* 2.610.

28 Herbert G. Wright, *Forty-six Lives Translated from Boccaccio's De Claris Mulieribus by Henry Parker, Lord Morley* (London, Oxford University Press, 1943) 156-159.

29 Francis L. Utley, *The Crooked Rib* (Columbus, Ohio State University, 1944) 219 (#236).

30 C. F. Fiske, *Vassar Medieval Studies* (New Haven, Yale University Press, 1923), 342-376.

31 Giuseppe Zonta, *Trattati del Cinquecento sulla Donna* (Bari, Laterza, 1913).

32 L. J. Walker, *Discourses of Niccolò Machiavelli* (New Haven, Yale University Press, 1950, 2 vol.), 1.464 (3.2.1) and 468 (3.5.1).

33 *Ibid.,* 1.539 (3.26.2).

34 Henry Bergen, *Lydgate's Fall of Princes* (London, Oxford University Press, 1927), part 4.161-170. The French and Latin texts are supplied.

35 The text of Laurent is given in Bergen, *op. cit.* (see note 34) 186.

36 Utley, *op. cit.* (see note 29) 266-268.

37 *Ibid.,* 272-276.

38 *Ibid.,* 124.

39 *Ibid.,* 160f.

40 Quintilian comments on the impressiveness of courage—a virtue customarily attributed to man by men—in women. Admirabilior in femina quam in viro virtus. The courage of Lucretia, he says, is more striking, for this very reason, than that of Cato and Scipio.

41 Carl J. Stratman, *Bibliography of Medieval Drama* (Berkeley, University of California Press, 1954) #2067; Paul Merker, "Die Anfänge der deutschen Barockliteratur," *Germanic Review* 6.109. See *A Bibliography of the Survival of the Classics, op. cit.* (see note 16) vol. 1.249 (#1031).

42 Hyder E. Rollins, *A Gorgeous Gallery of Gallant Inventions* (Cambridge, Harvard University Press, 1926) 63f.

43 T. W. Baldwin, *On the Literary Genetics of Shakspere's Poems and Sonnets* (Urbana, University of Illinois Press, 1950).

44 Douglas Bush, *Mythology and the Renaissance Tradition in English Poetry* (Minneapolis, University of Minnesota Press, 1932) 150.

45 There is a stereophonic recording of Shakespeare's *Lucrece* and other poems, released by the Shakespeare Recording Society, 461 Eighth Avenue, N.Y. 1.

46 Geoffrey Bullough, *Narrative and Dramatic Sources of Shakespeare* (New York, Columbia University Press, 1958), 2.405.

47 Allan Holaday, *Thomas Heywood's The Rape of Lucrece* (Urbana, University of Illinois Press, 1950) 12 in *Illinois Studies in Language and Literature,* vol. 34, #3. Other dramatic interpretations of the story were to follow. Rousseau mentions in his *Confessions* (book 8, in the year 1755) his plans for a tragedy in prose on Lucretia. Bernard Gagnebin and Marcel Raymond, *Jean Jacques Rousseau, Oeuvres Complètes* (Geneva, Librairie Gallimard, 1959), 394, 1459. The first two acts of this tragedy have been published. And in 1793 Rigobert Piquenard published a three-act tragedy in French verse entitled *Lucrece or Royalty Abolished.* Cf. British Museum, *Catalogue of Printed Books* (Ann Arbor, Edwards, 1946) vol. 42, col. 248.

48 Arthur M. Young, *Troy and Her Legend* (University of Pittsburgh Press, 1948) 58, 177.

49 Paul Schubring, *Cassoni* (Leipzig, Hiersemann, 1915 and 1923).

50 *Ibid.,* 223 (#21) and plate 3.

51 *Ibid.,* 368 (#644) and plate 138.

52 *Ibid.,* 278 (#261-263) and plate 58; and in supplement, #921f. on plate 11 and #898 on plate 2. Cf. also main volume, 338 (#492).

53 *Ibid.*, 289 (#304); and *The Burlington Magazine* 9 (1906), 291 and plate (p. 289).

54 *Ibid.*, 331 (#469) and plate 109.

55 *Ibid.*, 352 (#563) and plate 123.

56 *Ibid.*, 386 (#735) and plate 157.

57 Robert H. Cust, *Giovanni Antonio Bazzi* (London, Murray, 1906).

58 Schubring, *op. cit.* (see note 49), supplement, #924 on plate 13. For still another version of the story cf. Schubring, main volume, 384 (#727) and plate 154.

59 *Ibid.*, 271 (#208) and plate 46; 330 (#468) and plate 111; 357 (#579) and plates 130f.; and 379 (#697).

60 Adolfo Venturi, *North Italian Painting of the Quattrocento Lombardy, Piedmont, Liguria* (New York, Harcourt, Brace, 1931?), 50 and plate 36.

61 Giorgio Nicodemi, *Gerolamo Romanino* (Brescia, Società del Romanino, 1925).

62 George M. Richter, *Giorgio da Castelfranco* (Chicago, University Press, 1937), 337 (#1776, 1778, 1779).

63 Bernard Berenson, *Lorenzo Lotto* (New York, Phaidon, 1956), 99 and #241.

64 György Gombosi, *Palma Vecchio, Gemälde und Zeichnungen* (Berlin, Deutsche Verlags-Anstalt, 1937) 80, 97.

65 Sydney J. Freedberg, *Parmigianino* (Cambridge, Harvard University Press, 1950) 221f. and figures 118 a, b; and figure 119.

66 Frederick M. Clapp, *Jacopo Carucci da Pontormo* (New Haven Yale University Press, 1916) 179 (#75).

67 Seymour de Ricci, *Census of Medieval and Renaissance Manuscripts in the United States and Canada* (New York, Wilson, 1935, 3 vol.), i.827 (#418).

68 Hans Tietze, *Paolo Tintoretto* (New York, Phaidon, 1948), 354, 357, and figure 285.

69 Percy H. Osmond, *Paolo Veronese* (London, Sheldon, 1927), 97 and plate 59b.

70 Cosimus Stornajolo, *Codices Urbinates Latini* (Rome, Vatican, 1921), vol. 3, pp. 437f, #1571.

71 Bertina Suida Manning and William Suida, *Luca Cambiaso* (Milan, Ceschina, 1958), 132, 159, 188, and figures 343, 344, and 456.

72 Cesare Gnudi, *Guido Reni* (Florence, Vallecchi, 1955), 79 (#63) and plate 117.

73 *Ibid.*, 95 (#99) and plate 171.
74 *Ibid.*, 100 (#111) and plate 195.
75 Ellis Waterhouse, *Painting in Britain, 1530–1790* (Baltimore, Penguin, 1953), 91.
76 *Paintings and Sculpture from the Kress Collection* (Washington, D.C., National Gallery of Art, 1945), 137.
77 Curt Glaser, *Lukas Cranach* (Leipzig, Insel, 1921), 197, 209; Ed. Heyck, *Lukas Cranach* (Bielefeld, Velhagen and Klasing, 1927), 103 and figures 88, 89, 101; Max Friedlander and Rosenberg, *Die Gemälde von Lucas Cranach* (Berlin, Deutscher Verein, 1932) lists 35 Lucretias.
78 H. Tietze and E. Tietze Conrat, *Kritisches Verzeichnis der Werke Albrecht Dürers* (Basel, Holbein, 1937), Band ii, figures 359 and 702.
79 Erwin Panofsky, *Albrecht Dürer* (Princeton, University Press, 1943), ii.20 (#106) in Munich, and ii.96 (#932) in Vienna.
80 Carel van Mander, *Dutch and Flemish Painters* (New York, McFarlane, 1936), 544.
81 C. Hofstede De Groot, *A Catalogue Raisonné of the Most Eminent Dutch Painters of the Seventeenth Century* (London, Macmillan, 1916), vol. 6, p. 143 (#218), and p. 144 (#219, 220); and Emile Michel, *Rembrandt* (London, Heinemann, 1903), 381.
82 *Ibid.*, 6.144 (#220a).
83 Paul Kristeller, *Early Florentine Woodcuts* (London, Kegan Paul, 1897) xv, and p. 51 (cut 62).
84 Eugene Muntz, *Raphaël* (Paris, Hachette, 1881), 404, 407; and Pittaluga, *op. cit.* (see note 85), 144 and figure 77.
85 Mary Pittaluga, *L'incisione italiana nel cinquecento* (Milan, Hoepli, 1928), 159 and figure 95; and Arthur M. Hind, *Catalogue of Early Italian Engravings* (London, British Museum, 1910), 546.
86 F. W. Hollstein, *Dutch and Flemish Etchings, Engravings and Woodcuts* (Amsterdam, Hertzberger, 1949), vol. 10.152.
87 Howard Simon, *500 Years of Art and Illustration* (Cleveland, World Publishing Company, 1942), 14.
88 Hollstein, *op. cit.* (see note 86), vol. 13.214f.
89 Heinrich Göbel, *Wandteppiche*, vol. 1, *Die Niederlande* (Leipzig, Klinkhardt and Biermann, 1923), part 1.551; vol. 2, part 1, *Die Romanischen Länder* (1928), 194, 395; Phyllis Ackerman, *Tapestry the Mirror of Civilization* (New York, Oxford University Press, 1933), 92, 123, 124.

90 W. G. Thomson, *A History of Tapestry* (London, Hodder and
    Stoughton, 1906), 223, 248; and J. Denucé, *Antwerp Art-
    Tapestry and Trade* (The Hague, Nijhoff, 1936), 63f; and
    G. T. Van Ysselsteyn, *Tapestry Weaving in the Northern
    Netherlands* (Leiden, Uitgeversmaatschappij, 1936, 2 vol.),
    1.117 and 2.195 (#425).
91 Alfred Loewenberg, *Annals of Opera 1597–1940* (Geneva,
    Societas Bibliographica, 1943, 1955), col. 1435.
92 Bernard Rackham, *Early Netherlands Majolica* (London, Bles,
    1926), 66 and plate 9.
93 Giuseppi Liverani, *Five Centuries of Italian Majolica* (New
    York, McGraw, Hill, 1960), 33.
94 *Ibid.*, plate 50.
95 Bernard Rackham, *Catalogue of the Glaisher Collection of
    Pottery and Porcelain in the Fitzwilliam Museum, Cambridge*
    (Cambridge, University Press, 1935, 2 vol.), 1.258 (#2007).
96 *Ibid.*, 121 (#925).

Index

FIFTEENTH CENTURY ENGLAND

Percival Hunt   *(paper)* $2.95

A century in English history touched to life with the magic of a vivid and delicate style.

AL-FARABI'S SHORT COMMENTARY ON ARISTOTLE'S *PRIOR ANALYTICS*

Nicholas Rescher $3.00

Aristotle's *Prior Analytics*—the key work of his logical Organon—has been studied by philosophers and scholars for almost 2,000 years, but most of its significant Arabic interpretations have long been unavailable. The recent discovery of several Arabic manuscripts in Istanbul revealed the "Short Commentary on *Prior Analytics*" by the great medieval Islamic philosopher al-Farabi. Professor Rescher is the first scholar to translate this work into English. He has supplemented the translation with an informative introduction and numerous footnotes.

RASHI AND THE CHRISTIAN SCHOLARS

Herman Hailperin $15.00

A definitive study of some of the greatest biblical scholarship of the Middle Ages, this book illuminates the intellectual relations between Christians and Jews as revealed in the commentaries of Rashi (Rabbi Shelomo Izhaki), a French Jew, and Nicholas de Lyra, a French Franciscan, on their common religious inheritance—the Old Testament.

Dr. Hailperin, who is Rabbi of Pittsburgh's Tree of Life Congregation, has spent a lifetime on the research for this book, exploring the collections of seminaries and libraries in Europe and Jerusalem and corresponding with other scriptural scholars.